C. B. Greenfield: THE TANGLEWOOD MURDER

Lucille Kallen

WYNDHAM BOOKS : New York

ACKNOWLEDGMENT

I am indebted, and grateful, to some very kind and thoughtful people for their assistance in regard to technical details. My thanks to my good friends Dr. Martin Dolgin and Joy and Joel Rosen. Also to Gabriel Banat, Dr. Stuart Nevins, Stephen Arkin, Lorraine Lauzon, Frank Gullino, Betsy Schwartz, Victor Alpert, Sheldon Rotenberg, and Dr. D. E. Campbell.

For Florence Brooks Dunay and David Weisgal
who made it possible

NOTE: There is, of course, and thank God, an actual Tanglewood and an actual Boston Symphony Orchestra —two of the few remaining reasons for rejoicing—but I have absolutely no personal knowledge of the private lives or the personalities of any of the orchestra members, and those depicted here are, as are the other characters in this story, purely fictional creations. As to the locale and performances, I only regret that none of the words at my command has been adequate to convey their enchantment. The same regret applies to Wheatleigh.

L.K.

1

TANGLEWOOD, THE scenic summertime mecca of the music lover, sits midway along the western border of Massachusetts.

The village of Sloan's Ford, the suburban domicile of Charles Benjamin Greenfield, disgruntled crusader and publisher of the Sloan's Ford *Reporter,* occupies a more or less square mile approximately one hundred and twenty miles south and west of Tanglewood.

Among its many amenities, Tanglewood can draw on the security provided by a number of police contingents, including those of Lenox and Stockbridge and those supplied by the county of Berkshire.

It would, therefore, take a seer of considerable talent to predict that a crime culminating on the Tanglewood grounds would be tracked to its source by the soft-spoken gadfly of Sloan's Ford. And that it would, by extension, involve me.

There was certainly no intimation in the air, no bird of ill omen flew across my line of vision as I drove down Poplar Avenue that hot summer day, no portentous shiver touched my spine. I would, in fact, have welcomed a shiver of any kind; the two things uppermost in my mind were the heat, and the fact that while everyone else on the *Reporter* staff was preparing to take off for a change of scene, I saw no prospect of leaving town even for two consecutive days, let alone two weeks.

The Honda had been standing in the driveway, baking in the midsummer sun, and I was steering with two fingertips and trying to sit an inch off the sweltering seat as I drove. The few precious weeks of livable weather we call spring were long over; the miracle of crocus and daffodil and forsythia, the tender green of newborn leaves and virgin grass, had given way to flashier flowers and trees and lawn from which the first fine careless rapture had fled. It was just plain July.

I parked at the curb in front of the old white mansard-roofed house, then ran up the path to the shade of the long shallow porch and in through the front door to where it was dim and faintly cooler. From Greenfield's office on the second floor, the Bohemian humors of Dvorak's piano quintet floated down the narrow stairway, and from the ground floor office on my left, I heard Calli Dohanis's unmistakable hoarse voice.

"I am going to lie on the beach!" she was crowing. "Like a princess! For two weeks! I am not going to *move!* They will bring me rum collins every hour, and scampi and garlic butter! And my *husband* will take care of the kids for a change! And I'll buy a new bikini every *day!*"

I walked in. She was standing, her long bare arms spread wide, her head thrown back in anticipatory ecstasy, in the center of the crowded office, surrounded by cartons packed with future copies of the Sloan's Ford *Reporter,* drifts of newsprint, stacks of Justo-writer sheets, piles of memos, and scrappy heaps of unused cuts. There was only one clear space in the room and that was a neat little island around Helen Deutch's desk and chair, which had been swept and dusted and where Helen, her short chunky figure as summery as it would ever get in a matronly print blouse and teal blue skirt, was adjusting the plastic cover over her machine.

She eyed Calli in her pose of lyrical abandon, her strapless, fuschia-colored cotton tube and her stilt-like sandals, and said, in her good-common-sense voice, "You don't go to the Caribbean in the summertime. It's too hot, and then there are hurricanes."

"Wrong!" Calli's arm swept a batch of cuts into a waste-basket. "Wrong, wrong! They have perfect weather in July! *August* is when the hurricanes come!" She saw me and shouted, "Maggie! It's *vacation!*" and danced into the al-cove, where the refrigerator and hot plate punctuated their workday with cups of herb tea, bottles of low calorie soda, and containers of cottage cheese.

Helen gave me a smile of complicity; one sane person to another in the presence of a lunatic. "Well," she said with little hope, "let's hope she enjoys it."

"She's already enjoying it," I said. "Are you going to the Cape?"

"No, we decided to do something different this year. We're going to Montauk." Helen, the adventuress.

Calli, recklessly emptying the cupboard shelves into a gar-bage pail, held out a dusty box of Fig Newtons.

"You think these are still any good? I remember them sit-ting here since Christmas."

I picked one out of the box. It had all the delectable chew-iness of a bullet. "I think what you have here," I said, "is an archeological find." I dropped the box into the garbage pail. "Listen, I only came in to wish everybody bon voyage, but since you're still in a state of chaos, can I help with something?"

"No, no," Calli said, "the layout room is done, I cleaned it like a whistle. We'll soon be finished with the whole thing."

"Besides," Helen said with impeccable justice, "this is *our* job."

True. The ground-floor offices were the domain of Calli, who did the layout for the Sloan's Ford *Reporter*, and Helen, who did the typing. I, as superior and underpaid journalist, worked at home. In mid-July, before the *Reporter* closed down for two weeks, the three of us, plus Stewart Klein, who did the reporting I didn't do, and Charles Ben-jamin Greenfield, who, as I said, owned and edited and commanded and governed and reigned over the *Reporter*, all worked double time getting out two extra editions, mostly trivia, to be distributed in our absence for the pur-

pose of keeping the third-class mail rate. Then we were free
to turn our backs on the paper and run out to gambol in the
summer sun. Calli and Helen, however, had first to tidy up
and pack away.

Whether Greenfield—who, I assumed, was upstairs in his
office with his stereo—was also straightening up and packing
away, was doubtful; the mass of national and foreign
newspapers, magazines, books, files, clippings and corre-
spondence which always occupied the various derelict armchairs he kept there, and roamed over the enormous oak
desk and crammed itself onto the bookshelves and pushed
out of the not-quite-closed doors of the file cabinets, lent
credence to the theory that nothing in that room had been
tidied away since the second century.

That his office, however, like his living quarters on the
floor above, would be uninhabited for two weeks, was without doubt. Greenfield, also, would be running out to gambol in the sun. Not that he wanted to. Not that he looked
forward to vacations. He accepted them as hazards of the
trade. He endured them. Deprived of the comfortable and
congenial exigencies of his daily routine, he would sit out
the two weeks at a music festival. A widower, he had no
need to consult a wife's inclinations, and so he always attended a music festival.

He had been to Marlborough. He had been to Aspen. He
had braved the crowds at Spoleto. He had traversed London
from St. Paul's to the Royal Albert and the Royal Festival
Hall to listen to Barenboim and Neville Marriner, to the
Aeolian String Quartet, the London Philharmonic and the
Academy of St. Martin. He had even donned borrowed evening dress so that he wouldn't be thrown out of Glynde-
bourne. And once he'd paid the price of a January cold at
the height of summer, in the wind and rain of Edinburgh.
But most often, as this year, he headed north to the proven
elysium of Tanglewood.

I spared a moment for a little envy. Tanglewood, that serene, tree-shaded, grass-floored, mountain-ringed concert

hall under the Massachusetts sky. Nature's *Symphony Pastorale*.

"So where are you going, Maggie?"

"To the supermarket."

"I mean for *vacation*."

"That's where I'm going. To the supermarket. Elliot's going to spend two weeks playing tennis at the swim club and the boys both have jobs at Beef and Brew, or Ribs and Root Beer, or one of those elegant places. They're all going to be coming home at various hours like troops after a forced march, and someone has to keep the refrigerator stocked."

Calli looked horrified. *"No vacation?"*

"Well, you see, we got word that tuition next year will be going from merely prodigious to astronomical, so we had second thoughts. As soon as the boys are out of college, we'll fly off to exotic places. Always provided there are any left."

The street door opened and closed and C. B. Greenfield stood in the office doorway. Long and saturnine, with the face and posture of a cosmic repairman who has just inspected the world and isn't sure he can get the parts to fix it, his face was slightly flushed from exertion and a lock of his hair, like gray corn silk, stuck damply to his forehead.

I gaped at him and glanced involuntarily at the ceiling through which the quintet could still be heard.

"I thought you were up there!" I said.

Greenfield's eyes were also on the ceiling, and when he lowered them they rested on Calli: he knew Helen would never have the presumption to play his tapes in his absence.

"Dohanis," he said, in his quiet, benign, and totally deceptive manner, "your temerity doesn't surprise me. But your musical taste comes as something of a shock."

"Oh, don't worry!" Calli assured him. "I still think that itsy-pitsy music is for old ladies in rocking chairs, but that's the only kind you have up there and we had to celebrate vacation."

Greenfield's expression, which habitually covered the range from aggrieved to martyred, settled for long-suffering.

"To think," he muttered, turning away, "that Greece was the cradle of civilization." He started up the stairs, stopped, said, "Maggie," without looking at me, and continued upward.

"I told you not to," Helen said to Calli as she flicked dust off the plastic cover.

I followed Greenfield up the stairs to the office, which occupied the entire second floor, with Greenfield's huge desk and his noisy swivel chair against the windows overlooking the street. On his way to the desk he pushed at several tons of printed material engulfing one of the veteran armchairs, thereby clearing an area a good four inches in circumference.

"Sit down," he said, looking preoccupied, and subsided into his swivel chair. I chose to uncover the arm of the chair and perch on it.

"So," I said, "have a good time. Enjoy the music. I know it won't be easy, but bear in mind that two weeks go by very quickly, and before you know it you'll be free to go back to work."

He regarded the cuffs of his wilted cord trousers and said, "Do you realize that the population of Sloan's Ford has increased by seventy-five percent over the past thirty years?"

I looked at him carefully. It seemed an idle, casual observation, but having often experienced his devious approaches to a demand on my time and energy, I heard behind it the faint, far-off sound of a warning bell.

"Each family," he continued, "drives at least two cars; the traffic into and out of town has multiplied in direct proportion to the rising number of consumers, ditto the service vehicles, and the carbon monoxide level is no longer relatively innocuous."

I hazarded a guess. "You've moving to Maine."

"Be serious. I'm merely pointing out that it's mandatory, at least once a year, to breathe untainted air. Your health demands it."

"*My* health! Aha!" Light began to glimmer at the end of the tunnel. "What is it exactly you want me to do, Charlie?"

"If you had any regard for your lungs, you'd spend a few days in the mountains."

"The mountains!" It all came clear. "Something happened to the Plymouth!"

He sighed. "I didn't walk all the way back from the garage, in the sun, for the exhilaration of it. The Plymouth has a grave illness. Probably fatal."

This was a milestone to be recorded. Greenfield's solid, venerable, 1957 Plymouth—than which there was no more carefully maintained vehicle on earth—was finally succumbing to old age and death.

"My sympathies," I said, sincerely.

"How long is it since you've been to the Berkshires?"

"You really expect me to drive you all the way up there?"

"Two and a half hours to Massachusetts is not an expedition into the African interior. I doubt we'll need native bearers to carry the supplies."

"Charlie, you have three daughters and all of them can drive."

"One is in New Mexico, one is conducting summer classes at N.Y.U., and one has a child with a temperature." He paused. "You could hear a few rehearsals. Elliot could come. He's on vacation."

"Elliot is top-seeded in a tennis tournament at the swim club. He will go nowhere. There are people called Hertz and Avis who rent cars."

That was a pointless observation, I knew. Greenfield had once, years ago, rented a car when the Plymouth was in for minor surgery, and had left it in his garage the entire week. His faith and trust were not easily won; they had to be earned by long and loyal service. It had taken five years for him to accept that the Plymouth would probably get him where he wanted to go without falling apart. I knew, also, that Tanglewood could not be comfortably reached by train and that Greenfield would no more travel by bus than willingly submit to vivisection.

"I would naturally pay all expenses," he said. "They're

playing Brahms and Prokofiev this week." He paused again.
"And Ravel."

Ravel. I had long suspected that Greenfield made a list of
all my weaknesses and consulted it whenever he needed to
prey on them to achieve his own ends. He had once
suggested that while Ravel had an unrivaled genius for or-
chestration, he was not a superlative composer, and I had
walked out of the office never to return, for two whole days.

Tanglewood. And not only Brahms and Prokofiev, but
Ravel.

I told him it was out of the question because of Elliot and
the boys and keeping the refrigerator stocked.

He told me that was nonsense and that he had already
called the place where he'd be staying and they were holding an extra room.

"And as for the other considerations," he added, frowning
at a blue jay pecking at seeds he had scattered on the windowsill for smaller birds, "you can assure your husband that
my intentions are, for the moment, blameless." He picked up
his horn-rimmed glasses from the desk and polished them on
the front of his loose shirt. "Of course, what *your* intentions
are, I can't say."

I suppressed a smile. Our firmly established relationship,
consisting of equal parts of comfortable friendship, grudging respect, and simple exasperation, and our mutual un-
willingness to disturb a workable status quo, was such that
neither he nor I nor Elliot would give a second thought to
the possible consequences of our going off to stay in the
same hotel for three or four days. The fact that we each
belonged to a different sex only surfaced when Greenfield
occasionally reached the height of innuendo by remarking
that I was "too argumentative for dalliance" or that I
"lacked the talent for graceful submission."

He had "someone," somewhere. I'd seen evidence of it—
for instance a hand-knit sweater on his birthday (and none
of his daughters would be caught dead with a knitting
needle) or his question to Helen as to where she'd bought
the fur-lined boots she wore all winter (and none of his

daughters would walk out of the house in those boots). I imagined "someone' as a juicy fifty, calm, self-sufficient, undemanding, and nobody's fool. But I'd never know; he kept that lady and that corner of his life quite separate.

"You could always keep your door locked," I suggested.

"I'll trust you not to be importunate." He turned to his desk and began to sort the indecipherable memos he had scribbled to himself. "Rehearsal begins at ten A.M. We'll have to leave at seven-thirty to make it."

I said that if I was doing the driving, eight A.M. was as early as I was prepared to start. He said something about corruption and absolute power. I got up and started for the stairs. I had tried for years to have the last word in a conversation with Greenfield, but without success. I tried again.

I said, "I'll pick you up at eight-oh-five," and ran down the stairs. His voice came after me. "Fill the tank tonight."

Hopeless. I said goodbye to Helen and Calli and sped to the supermarket to buy three days' worth of provisions for my family, which included our golden retriever, George, who, I knew, would immediately lie down, devastated, with his head on his paws and his great reproachful eyes fixed on me, the minute I took a suitcase from the closet.

I had decided, inasmuch as Greenfield was footing the bill, to gorge myself on music and mountains until Friday.

Needless to say, it never entered my mind that the tranquil Berkshire countryside would be sprinkled not only with plaintive pianissimos and fiery fortés, not only with daisies, buttercups, and Queen Anne's lace, but also with riddles, secrets, passions, and an inexplicable corpse.

2

WE ROLLED along, the following morning, with our two suit-cases in the hatchback section of the Honda and Greenfield beside me in the passenger seat wearing chinos, a blue-and-white-checked sportshirt, and an air of resignation.

Conversation was minimal until we approached a convergence of main parkways.

"Straight ahead," Greenfield said.

"Straight ahead?"

"Straight ahead."

"If I don't take this exit I don't get on the Taconic!"

"We're not taking the Taconic."

"That's the only way I know!"

"Maggie. Straight ahead."

Teeth clenched, I went straight ahead.

"I only hope you know where you're going," I said crisply, "because I haven't the faintest idea how to get there from here."

"It's a sad commentary on your character," he said with appropriate sadness, "that you're so reluctant to put your trust in anyone's judgment but your own."

This from a man who steps outside with his eyes on the sky and the palm of his hand held out, after you've just told him it's stopped raining. So be it. Whatever happened now, it was his responsibility.

I found myself on Route 22 and eventually we passed Brewster, and some time beyond that it began to feel like real country: sun slanting through a tangle of trees, glinting on brown ponds and silver silos, and far off on the horizon, the smoky silhouettes of mountains.

To distract him from the prospect of two weeks' enforced relaxation, I began to hum.

"What," he asked glumly, "is that?"

"Ibert's *Paris Suite.*"

"Sounds more like 'Singin' in the Rain' to me."

"I thought you had an educated ear," I grumbled, and stopped humming.

He turned his face toward the window, closing down communication. I took a deep breath. And then, with pleasure, another. "You're right, Charlie," I said, "this doesn't smell like suburbia. It's either unpolluted or someone's been waving a giant wildflower deodorizer around here."

He gave me nothing but the back of his head, the wispy gray hair lifting in the breeze from the open window.

We sped through Dutchess County, into hills, between outcroppings of rock, past farmland dotted with black and white cows—an untidy, informal countryside and much more interesting, I had to admit (though I didn't), than the beautifully manicured Taconic. Greenfield broke his silence only to steer me in the right direction when necessary. And then it happened.

We were about ten miles this side of Sharon, Connecticut, when we saw, not far ahead, a girl standing casually in the middle of the highway, watching our speedy approach with bland unconcern and no noticeable intention of moving.

The reason was immediately apparent. A new-looking twodoor compact was standing on the verge with its hood up and a woman staring helplessly at its insides.

I had braked, of course, at the same moment that Greenfield muttered "*Merde!*" and now I pulled off the road, got out, and walked over to the two women.

They had been fashioned by the same designer: slender, long-legged, with soft, round, pretty faces. The older one, about forty, wore a sleeveless lavender cotton dress that I might have been able to afford at the end of the season, marked down. The one who'd been standing in the road was in her late teens, and whatever she was wearing undoubtedly came from the East Village. The older one looked up as I approached, with a total lack of expression. She had very large, surprised-looking eyes, the amber irises completely surrounded by white, the white completely surrounded by spiky mascaraed lashes, like two daisies with black petals, side by side. The rest of her face was extraordinarily smooth and blank, as though not once in forty years had she frowned, wept, screamed, or laughed.

"What's wrong with it?" I asked.

She spoke in a languid murmur. "The son of a bitch," she said, "overheated."

The younger one looked at me from behind huge dark glasses under a tangle of shoulder-length curls the color of dark honey, parted her small, soft lips, and said, "General Motors strikes again."

"Maybe the fan belt broke," I suggested, and looked into the greasy interior.

Greenfield, with the most grudging goodwill possible, had followed me, and as he came up to the car, the older woman's face was instantly transformed. She gave him a dazzling smile.

"Would you take a look?" she asked him.

I resented that deeply. I knew as much as Greenfield, if not more, about automobile engines. Which is to say, next to nothing.

With weary patience, Greenfield put a hand on each fender and peered at the oily machinery.

"The fan belt," he said, "is broken."

"Terrific," the girl said.

The older one said, "It's rented." Greenfield gave me a sidelong glance to mark this justification of his prejudice against rented cars, looked up and down the deserted road in a vain search for deliverance, and finally sighed. "We'd better give you a lift to Sharon. There should be a mechanic available there."

They took their shoulder bags from the car and the

younger one reached into the back seat and picked up something that turned out to be a tawny cat.

Greenfield threw me a pained look and started back to the Honda. I was tempted to ask what he had had against the Taconic, but refrained. The older woman locked the car and we all followed Greenfield and piled in, the two women and the cat in the back seat. As I started up, the rearview mirror showed me the older woman taking a hairbrush from her bag and running it through her feathery, copper-colored hair with long, lingering strokes.

There were introductions in which Greenfield took no part whatever. They were mother and daughter, which was no great surprise. Eleanor Springer and her daughter, Jenny.

"What's the cat's name?" I asked, to be agreeable.

"She's not really a cat," Jenny said, "she's an Egyptian princess. A descendant of Nefertiti. Also called Nefertiti. She was stolen in the dead of night from beside a pyramid where she used to sit in a golden dress watching the moon. She was given immortality by the magician Xantherpes who later became a standup comedian in Beverly Hills with a thousand-foot swimming pool, but the pool didn't do Nefertiti any good because he had turned her into a cat. She ran away and we found her wandering on Forty-second Street, so we took her home, because Forty-second Street is no place for a decent cat."

She said all this in a very calm, matter-of-fact voice, and Greenfield turned dismissively to stare out the window with shoulders that said he had given up hope of a safe and sane journey.

"Thank God you came along," Eleanor said in her enervated voice: "we've been standing there for hours."

"Twenty minutes," Jenny said.

"There must have been a dozen cars going by," Eleanor continued, delicately. "You think those bastards would stop? Every man for himself."

"How far are you going?" I asked.

"Lenox," she said.

"Stockbridge," Jenny said.

There was a sound, a kind of aborted moan, from Greenfield's window.

"Near Tanglewood," Eleanor murmured. "I want to watch Sorrel conduct the Brahms." The voice became barely audible. "He's the only sexy conductor left."

Over the miles we learned, without asking, that Eleanor came up to the Tanglewood area every summer, sometimes with Jenny, sometimes without, that she was divorced from Dr. Springer, who was a surgeon on Long Island, that she and Jenny lived in Manhattan "in an expensive ghetto," and that Eleanor, in her younger days, had spent a summer studying at Tanglewood.

"Just auditing," she said, "I was really studying water-color with an artist who taught in a barn behind the Tangle-wood students' dorm—they housed them in that private boys' school up the road . . . and I thought there must be some connection between music and painting . . . so I decided to audit Bernstein's classes at Tanglewood. . . ." The voice became a little breathless. "I used to hitch rides there . . . a lot of good-looking boys at Tanglewood . . . I remember one day Bernstein came to class with a white dinner jacket hanging from one finger. 'Who wants this?' he said. You should have seen the faces. . . ." The voice trailed off. "Sorrel was there that summer. . . ."

"I think Nefertiti has to pee," Jenny said.

"Oh . . ." Eleanor sounded unwilling to deal with this new crisis. "I guess she'll have to wait."

"You can get terrible bladder trouble from waiting," Jenny said placidly. "There was a girl at school who was thin as a rail but she never went to the bathroom because she was afraid of missing things, and she blew up from retained fluid until she weighed two hundred pounds. She was originally brought up in a convent in South America and she had a brother who danced flamenco. He was gay."

"That's ridiculous," Eleanor murmured.

"Which part?" asked Jenny obligingly, as though quite prepared to change whatever didn't suit.

Greenfield shifted slightly at his window and I stifled a

laugh. Eventually we arrived at Sharon, Connecticut, a posh and well-groomed little town, and located a garage. I waited while Eleanor wandered off, her mouth rehearsing the dazzling, helpless smile, to confer with a young mechanic with greasy hands and overalls, and Jenny let the cat loose in some roadside shrubbery.

Greenfield had the look of a man hanging onto patience by his fingernails.

"If we don't dawdle," he enunciated with great precision, "we can still make the rehearsal." Meaning don't be a dunce and offer to wait and see if they need a lift to Lenox.

Eleanor returned to announce that the greasy young mechanic would drive them back to their car in a tow truck and replace the fan belt, and to thank us, in her abstracted way, for our help.

As we left the garage, I saw the two women and the cat climbing into the high front seat of the dirty tow truck with the grease-covered mechanic, and I observed a moment of silence for the dainty lavender dress.

We continued on, up Route 44, past turn-of-the-century houses with deep porches, delectable Saratoga Gothic, and onto Undermountain Road with the Appalachian Trail undulating high against the sky on the left.

Greenfield finally broke the restful silence.

"I'm sure that your liberated hackles will rise," he said, "nevertheless it's a fact that there are women in the world who should not be allowed to run loose without a restraining male presence in the vicinity."

It was against my principles to agree, but he had a point. There was some archaic kind of femininity about Eleanor Springer, something that belonged to an earlier cultural pattern. She reminded me of a pampered show dog who has lost its master on Fifth Avenue and is elegantly and distractedly dodging traffic because it hasn't the sense to know why the red and green lights are there.

"However," I said, "the daughter is another story."

"The daughter," he said, "is science fiction."

"She's a little bizarre, but very bright. I kind of like her."

"Fortunately the matter is academic. With any luck we won't run into them again."

I wish I could say that at that moment I had a presentiment, but I did not. All I had at that moment was a passionate desire to get out from under the roof of that car and run through the fields.

We went up Route 7 to Stockbridge at top speed and followed the signs to Tanglewood, Greenfield sitting very still, an act that in someone else might have translated into the biting of nails. It was 10:47 when we got to the main gate, which meant Greenfield had missed almost an hour of the morning's rehearsal, and he was out of the car before the key was out of the ignition, rushing into the office where his friend Shura Charnov, a cellist with the orchestra, had left two passes in his name.

You do not need a pass to get into the Tanglewood grounds during the week, but you do need one to sit in the open-sided Music Shed. I had no desire to sit in the Music Shed. As Greenfield hurried me in that direction I looked wistfully at the lawn, something like a hundred luscious green acres of cropped grass lying in and out of the scattered shade of hickory, pine, mountain ash, and copper beech, inviting the body to stretch out and dream. You could hear every note of music perfectly from any place on that lawn, as a romantic passage from the Brahms Fourth floating out to us confirmed, but Greenfield had to *see* as well.

Rows of benches stood outside along each flank of the Music Shed for the use of casual music lovers strolling by who had the impulse to sit for a while and listen, but inside the Shed, in regular auditorium seats with a roof over their heads, a group of students, a few loyal orchestra wives, and a scattering of other people with passes sat down front in a section reserved for them. We bypassed the outdoor benches and Greenfield presented the passes to the monitor who came toward us treading softly, glanced at the passes, nodded importantly, and allowed us to take seats in the third row.

Up on the podium Jan Sorrel was thrusting his baton hither and yon at the hundred and six members of the incomparable Boston Symphony Orchestra. I looked him over critically, having just been briefed by Eleanor that he was loaded with sexuality. What I saw was a slightly taller than average man with a head that Michelangelo might have sculpted if he'd gone in for middle-aged models. His body movements had the kind of extravagant energy typical of highly competitive boys who prove themselves in sports, his hair should have been gray or graying but was uniformly golden and shaped long enough to cover his ears, and he wore a youthful sky-blue turtleneck shirt and well-cut slacks. He looked capable of being both charming and ruthless, which was, of course, attractive, but he also looked humorless, which killed it. On the whole, I decided, Eleanor was indulging in wishful thinking.

My eyes roamed over the cello section to find Shura Charnov. There he was. Round face, gray goatee, red shirt, his eyes all but closed under half-moon eyebrows and his mouth curved in a private, blissful smile as he sawed away. Shura and Greenfield were old friends from the days when Greenfield had labored in the vineyards of NBC News. They had met at the TV coverage of a Presidential musical event in Washington, and I had met Shura and his wife, Nadia, the year before when the Boston was playing Carnegie Hall. Greenfield had invited them to dinner, along with Elliot and me and Gordon Oliver (with whom Greenfield and I played weekly chamber music, weakly). Gordon's wife, Shirley, and I had prepared the dinner. Greenfield had provided the raw materials, the kitchen, the dining room, and the advice. It was nice to see Shura again. He was a warm-hearted and thoroughly impractical fellow.

I relaxed and edged my feet out of my canvas espadrilles. The sound of the orchestra was glorious; full, rich, and vivid. The stage lights glinted on the burnished wood of the string instruments and winked off the brasses. A bird, jealous, flew into the Shed, perched on the round clock high on the stage wall, listened critically for a moment, and flew out again, over our heads and on toward the blue mountains surrounding us. The air smelled of cut grass and flowers. Brahms soared into the stratosphere. It might not be paradise, but it would do.

One hour and eleven minutes later, precisely as the big hand on the wall clock touched the dot of 12:30, the music stopped, in the middle of a phrase.

"Good God!" I breathed, "they stopped on a dominant seventh. It's like an old joke."

"Union rules," Greenfield said, standing up. "Written in concrete. Let's go."

"Lunch?" I asked hopefully.

"To see Shura."

He made his way to the left across the auditorium. I followed him out and around the side of the Shed to a grassy area adjacent to the musicians' locker rooms. Musicians were emerging two by two, like surviving species from the Ark. Two horn players, two clarinetists, two second violins . . . This, of course, was pure fantasy. There was no way of knowing who belonged to what instrument; a few of them carried cases, some were empty-handed, and it was beyond me to distinguish violin case from viola, or flute case from clarinet.

Finally Shura appeared, in his fire-engine red shirt and faded blue slacks, talking animatedly to another musician who was nodding his head lethargically as they descended the few stairs to the grass. Then Shura caught sight of us, threw his arms wide, and hurried over.

Greenfield put out his hand but Shura ignored it and hugged him. To think I had lived to see the day when someone dared to hug C. B. Greenfield! A man, yet. Then he hugged me.

"What a surprise, Maggie Rome!"

"My car broke down, and Maggie was coming up for a few days anyway, so we drove up together," Greenfield said smoothly. "How is Nadia?"

"In perfect health, she's dying to see you. Tonight—*basta!* —we're booked to go to some people for dinner. You must absolutely come for dinner tomorrow, both of you, but today, later this afternoon, come for a drink. We have a short rehearsal this afternoon. Six o'clock—that's okay? You know how to get to the house?"

"Certainly," Greenfield said.

"In case you forgot, let me write down the directions."

"I remember perfectly," Greenfield insisted.

While Shura was writing down the driving directions on the back of an old shopping list I'd dug out of my bag, I eavesdropped on the musicians passing by.

". . . new recording of the Ninth. Tremendous."

"I'm not listening to any more Ninths. I've O.D.'d on Ninths."

"Haven't seen him for years. I hear he's playing at Irish wakes and bar mitzvahs."

"Don't tell the kid what to do with his life. Dvorak's father wanted him to be a butcher."

". . . played me a tape of this symphonic poem he composed. It sounded like a rock group sight-reading Mahler."

"Everybody makes rules. Brahms wanted a law passed to prevent violin concertos from beginning with an adagio. If the rule stinks, break it."

This last commandment was handed down by a man with a violin case who then blithely detached himself from a colleague and came over to us.

"Ah, Noel!" Shura said, pronouncing it *Noll*, "meet my friends, Charles Benjamin Greenfield, and Mrs. Maggie Rome. This is Noll Damaskin, my neighbor, my car pool, unfortunately a violinist, but what can you do."

Noel Damaskin laughed and said, "The only thing a cellist hates more than a violinist is a bass player." He shook hands with Greenfield, turning to me at the same time with a nod and a boyish smile, saying, "Delighted, delighted." He was in his early forties, vigorous, sleek, tanned, well cared for, with handsome gray eyes and a spectacular set of teeth, beautifully displayed when he smiled his frank, friendly smile, which he did a lot. He had the kind of tumbled hair that women supposedly lust to run their hands through. It was the color of tobacco, with a silver streak right where it did the most good.

"Did you hear the rehearsal?" he asked. "The Brahms is stupendous, isn't it? Of course, all those triple fortés Sorrel seems to want—I don't know what he thinks he's doing—did you notice, Shura? Sounds like *Götterdämmerung*. I wish *I* had that stick in my hand. Oh by the way"—this to Shura alone, in a more confidential tone—"I suppose you heard there was another—um—incident?"

Shura's face clouded. "Yes," he said. "Terrible."

At that moment a stubby index finger poked viciously at Damaskin's arm. It belonged to a big, heavy man in his sixties with some sparse white hair around the edges of a pink scalp, thick eyeglasses separated at the bridge by a fleshy nose, and a slit of mouth between pendulous jowls.

"I was *not* down-bowing!" he declared gutturally, his jowls quivering with anger, "and stop trying to make me look bad! I was playing Brahms before you had a tooth in your head!" He trundled off in the direction of the lawn, his thick shoulders hunched.

"Holchek!" Damaskin called after him, "it was a *joke*, Holchek!" But Mr. Holchek kept walking. Damaskin shook his head. "Paranoid," he said, and glanced at his watch—it was one of those that give you the latest Dow-Jones average and the current temperature in every corner of the world— and put a hand on Shura's shoulder. "Look, you want to spend some more time with your friends, I can probably get a lift with—"

"No, no," Shura said, "I have to go home. Nadia's waiting for the car."

"Then I'll meet you in the parking lot. I just want a word with Sandy." He flashed the teeth at us, said he hoped to see us again, and strode off.

"What terrible incidents," Greenfield asked, "was he talking about?"

Shura frowned. "There's some funny business going on, Charlie. You remember Batista, the bassoonist, I introduced you last year? He has a house with a deck in the back—

cantilevered—four days ago it collapsed. Just pure luck Batista and his wife were not home, otherwise they sit there all the time. Then—you know Tsuji? Flutist? No, you never met him. Two nights ago he was driving back from South Lee, late at night, a car forced him off the road into a ditch, he nearly lost control of the car and turned over. This morning, one of the girls—a second violinist—got a threatening letter in the mail—you know, one of those things with cutout letters from a newspaper. 'You better watch out.' Something like that." He sighed and said, "It's beginning to look very funny. Very funny."

"Shura," Greenfield said, "when these things happen to other people, they're called coincidence. When they happen to a Russian, they constitute a plot."

"How many years have I been in this country? Almost thirty years. This has nothing to do with Slavic temperament; the whole orchestra is getting nervous, talking about a jinx on the BSO. *One* incident—maybe. *Two* incidents— could still be coincidence. *Three*—!" He shook his head. "Well, I have to go, Nadia will bite my head off. Don't forget, six o'clock. You have the directions? Good."

Shura's stocky figure plodded off down the path to the parking lot, and Greenfield watched him go. For the first time in two days he did not look restless.

"*Now* lunch?" I asked.

"Mmm," he said, and we started off across the lawns to the cafeteria, the pudgy figure of Holchek, far ahead of us, clutching a sheaf of music in one hand.

Under the wide-spreading trees on the lawn bordering the cafeteria, students sprawled on the grass with their containers of yogurt, their instruments and music sheets, some of them practicing quietly on flute or clarinet, some holding intense or lackadaisical conversations, others playing with a Frisbee. There was a combined scent of grass and trees and flowers and food in the balmy, sunny air, and I was ravenous.

I piled my tray with a bowl of gazpacho, a dish of tuna salad, a large red apple, a huge oatmeal cookie, and a con-

tainer of milk. Greenfield, holding his chopped egg sandwich and coffee, regarded me with mild astonishment.

"The country air?" he inquired.

"That, and six hours since breakfast."

We took our trays out to a roofed area extending from the
cafeteria proper, open on three sides and containing long
wooden tables and benches, most of them overflowing with
students. Here and there a grayer or less abundantly en-
dowed head of hair indicated that members of the faculty
were also lunching.

We made our way to a distant table only partially occupied at one end by three very slender and beautiful boys
who looked Haitian. They had curving spines like the stalks
of flowers that have grown too tall, and spoke some melodic
but totally incomprehensible language. We sat down at the
far end of the table and I dealt simultaneously with gazpacho and the scene around me.

At the next table a blond Adonis in a tie-dyed T-shirt was
holding forth on the relative merits of harmonic progression
as prescribed by Persichetti and Walter Piston, while a plain
Jane with lank brown hair and steel-rimmed glasses listened
avidly, cheek cupped in her hand. Beside them a very short,
bearded young man in a navy sweatshirt with a sandwich
and an open score in front of him was absorbed in conducting the score, using the straw from his milk carton as a
baton. A lanky redhead at another table had his nose in a
book entitled *Manual Practique,* and a trio of girls—one with
a face from a Botticelli painting, one plump and depressed
in tight jeans, and one very forthright and Midwestern who
needed a horse to complete her—shrieked and whispered and
occasionally looked around to see if anyone was watching.

I took a bite of the large red apple and said to Greenfield,
"Imagine being twenty years old and spending the summer
with nothing to do but play music all day, out here with the
trees and the mountains and the sunshine. . . ."

"And intense competition and constant pressure to per-
form."

"It still beats working in a cotton mill. I hope they know how blessed they are."

He took a sip of coffee. "It always takes twenty years to realize you were once blessed."

The Botticelli girl stood up and looked around, her hair falling to her shoulders like a fountain of dull gold. The plump one pantomimed maidenly distress.

"Oh where is he, where is my love?" she moaned.

"Come on, Allison," said the forthright midwest, "tell us who it is."

"Keep it up," said Botticelli, "and I'll put soap in your flute. Let's go, it's one thirty."

I turned to Greenfield. "It's one thirty," I said, "and I've been sitting for the better part of five and a half hours. I have to get some exercise."

He waved toward the lawn. "You have several acres. Run around it."

"In this heat? What I need is a swim. My kingdom for an Olympic-size pool. A reasonable sum for anything smaller." I looked at him quickly in sudden apprehension. "This place you've booked into does have a pool?"

"First lunch, now a pool," he muttered. "Is there no end to your demands?" He got up and walked out onto the lawn, leaving his paper plate and cup behind. I gathered our debris and took it to the receptacle provided for such things.

When I caught up to him I said, "Seriously. Does it have a pool?"

"If it does," he said with impeccable logic, "you'll know soon enough. If it doesn't, there's nothing you can do about it. It's a pointless question."

I knew he knew whether or not the place had a pool. There were only two possible reasons for his refusal to tell me. Either it was one of those dreary genteel little guest houses smelling of furniture polish and broccoli with no room around it for anything but a bed of petunias, and he didn't want to admit it, or he was merely being intractable as a way of enlivening these hours of enforced idleness.

I could only hope it was the latter.

In the parking lot I unlocked the car and slid behind the wheel. The seat was a furnace. The wheel scorched my hands.

"Which way to the mausoleum?" I asked.

"Go straight ahead to the fork in the road and bear left onto West Hawthorne. The Inn is a mile or so down the road."

"Oh, an Inn! I do hope," I said nicely, "it has indoor plumbing."

He was silent for about thirty seconds, just long enough for me to think that I had finally, after all, had the last word.

Then he said, "You're assuming it has an indoors."

3

IT WAS not an Inn, it was not a guest house, it was not a motel, it was a little summer hideaway for Marie Antoinette and a few dozen of her closest friends.

When we had gone a mile or so along West Hawthorne, Greenfield instructed me to turn left onto a dirt road, and I thought, "Camp Prickly Heat, here we come." The tree-lined road wound past a single tennis court on our left and a sweep of lawn on the right. Then it turned, stunningly, unbelievably, into a fountained courtyard with a gravel drive that curved around the fountain to a porte cochere sheltered by an ornate glass-and-wrought-iron marquee.

On either side of the wide front steps huge terra cotta urns big enough to take a bath in were filled with vivid red geraniums. There were high arched doors with a long Florentine balcony above them, and two tall, incredibly beautiful Tiffany windows to one side, a pillared portico on the left, a glimpse of gardens beyond, all of this attached to a chateau of biscuit-colored brick designed by someone in love with sixteenth-century Italian architecture. It sat among acres of lawns, trees, and terraces against a background of purple-green mountains, blue sky, and tiny white puffs of cloud.

Fortunately, I braked before the car went up the stairs and in through the arched doors.

Wheatleigh, I subsequently discovered, was well known to hundreds of regular Berkshire vacationers, but while I'd spent many an afternoon and evening at Tanglewood concerts, I'd come and gone in the space of a day, and never knew that slightly off the beaten path there stood such a silken retreat.

I was still sitting mesmerized before this Palladian palace when Greenfield hauled the suitcases out of the hatchback and matter-of-factly handed them to the boy in the dark slacks and short-sleeved white shirt who had appeared at the sound of the car. I stepped tentatively out of the car as Greenfield slammed the hatchback and dabbed at his forehead with a handkerchief. He might have been checking into some mountain cabin in the Catskills.

We went up the steps and entered a sumptuous Hall, rising forty feet to the ceiling of the second floor, from which a gallery looked down at us and which was reached by a wide Grand Staircase sweeping elegantly past the Tiffany windows. In the Hall, a long sofa and deep wing chairs flanked an enormous fireplace, sunlight splashed on gleaming oak herringbone floors, and at the far end, sixty feet away through a series of French doors, there was a glimpse of umbrella tables adorning a spacious terrace.

I said in a low voice, "I wonder what the peasants are doing tonight."

The boy, whose eyes and nose peeped out from between equally luxuriant black hair and beard, set the bags down and asked Greenfield if he wanted to check in. Greenfield said he knew where the office was, and disappeared down a corridor to the right, past a huge, ornate gilt frame standing on an easel, which contained not a painting, but a velvet bulletin board. I wandered over. I am a bulletin-board addict. Like those people who can't resist free samples of some new spread they're handing out on crackers in the supermarket, no matter how unappetizing, I find it impossible to pass up free information.

This board had attached to it various notices of local attractions, including the week's programs at Tanglewood, Jacob's Pillow, and the Berkshire Playhouse, a corner earmarked for messages, and a tennis roster with names penciled in for different hours of the day. Nine to ten, Polk–Sturman. Ten to eleven, Gornick–Halper. Five to six, Sorrel.

Sorrel! How many Sorrels could there be within walking distance of Tanglewood? It must be! Fancy staying at the same palazzo as the guest conductor of the Boston Symphony. It wasn't going to be easy going back to stock the refrigerator, after this.

Greenfield returned with room keys and I pointed to Sorrel's name on the tennis roster. He nodded.

"Last year, Bernstein was staying here."

Trust him to top it.

"This place is not as big as it seems," he said. "More flora than fauna. I booked my room long ago, and I was lucky to be able to wheedle one for you at this late date. I don't know how adequate it'll be."

I didn't care. An old linen cupboard would do.

He handed the boy the key to my room and said to me, "I'm down that way—One C," and went off to his room down a corridor leading left off the Hall.

I followed the young man with the beard up the Grand Staircase, past the Tiffany windows, along the wide carpeted gallery decorated with bowls of flowers on antique tables and framed prints of Rembrandt etchings, down some steps, around a corner into a narrow corridor, and there I was—the linen cupboard.

Small it was, but instantly endearing. Fresh, clean, blue and white, it had a tiny fireplace, a comfortable single bed, and casement windows with filmy white curtains moving in the breeze. It was Louisa May Alcott and I loved it.

I suddenly remembered I had a crucial question and asked the beard, who was standing there watching my reaction with a fond, proprietorial smile.

"Of course," he said. "You go back down the stairs, across the Hall to the far side, there's a door there on your left that opens out onto the front portico, from there you go down the path to the bottom of the garden, and there's the pool." He grinned, fingered his beard, accepted a tip, and left, and five minutes later, wearing my bikini and terrycloth robe, I stood warily in the gallery, looking down the imposing sweep of the staircase and wondering what to do next. It was all very well to say "go back down the staircase and across the Hall"—but in a terrycloth robe and rubber thongs? What if Marie Antoinette came into view? What if *Sorrel* did?

I desperately regretted not having asked the beard to show me the back way out of this palace. There must be one. Surely the chambermaids didn't go romping up and down the Grand Staircase carrying mops and Ajax?

I no sooner had the thought than a large, sunburnt woman with straw-colored hair came undulating up the staircase in a bikini, a short, open coverup, and clogs with five-inch heels. Oh, well, I decided, if informality is the keynote . . . Nevertheless, I ran down and across the Hall in record time and felt more comfortable when I reached the dimness of the corridor leading to Greenfield's room and the exit to the portico. I knocked on the door.

"It's me, Charlie. I'm going to the pool."

He opened the door and my affection for the little blue-and-white room was immediately alienated. This was a vast, ivory-colored room, shining with light from the French doors, boasting a six-foot-high fireplace with carved white mantel bedecked with cupids and garlands, a wide bed canopied and quilted in white, two tall, narrow, white-and-gilt French lingerie chests, white wicker armchairs on either side of a gilt wicker table, a small sea of rug in soft greens and browns, a marble-topped chest, a small green tree growing in a white pot in one corner, and beyond the French doors, a private balcony. I was certain it had been transported intact from the Raffles Hotel in Singapore, lacking only Rita Hayworth lying on the bed. I offered to forego any raises in salary for the next five years in exchange for a switch of rooms.

"You call that an offer?" he said scornfully.

I ran my fingers over the white wicker. "You might have warned me about this place."

"To what end?"

"I would have packed my crown jewels. Or at least my Adidas running shoes."

"People of character don't allow the environment to dictate their style."

"I never claimed to have character. Just beauty, brains, talent, and greed. I wonder who built the place. It looks like a set for a Bergman film. The only people I've seen so far are the beard and a lady with lots of tanned skin. They both look as though they'd been sent over from Central Casting."

Greenfield took a pile of socks from his suitcase and transferred it impatiently to an open drawer of the marble-topped chest. "It was built," he said, "by the man who was responsible for the construction of the Erie Railroad."

"I'm glad he changed his style before he started this."

Greenfield was not in the mood for levity. He moved some shirts from suitcase to chest and said, "His name was H. H. Cook, he was the grand-nephew of an English baronet. He had four daughters, one of whom evidently wanted to be a countess, so papa allowed her to marry Carlos de Heredia, a Cuban with the appropriate title. Cook then bought two hundred and fifty acres of land from Gideon Northrup Smith, grandson of a pro-British Tory who ran a tavern during the American Revolution. You are standing on the site of that tavern. Cook built this house, in the style of an Italian villa, and his daughter, the Countess de Heredia, lived here until she died in 1946, after which her two nieces sold the estate to a real estate dealer from Chicago, who then sold the house and twenty-one acres to the Boston Symphony, and they in turn sold it, and so on."

A Cuban countess living in an Italian villa on the site of a Yankee tavern owned by a pro-British Tory who was plotting to abort the American Revolution. It sounded like a story Jenny Springer might have dreamed up. "How do you know all this?" I asked him.

He paused with a pair of green-and-white striped pajamas in his hand, raised one bushy eyebrow, and said, "I read." He pushed the pajamas into a drawer.

"Well, I don't know whether to thank Mr. Cook or the Countess or the Boston Symphony, but someone apparently built a pool, and I'm going to swim in it. Are you?"

"I haven't decided." He looked fretful and restless again.

I left him to make the difficult decision in solitude and crossed the corridor to the door the beard had mentioned, which opened on the front portico with its Roman balustrades and another enormous old terra cotta urn, this one full of a thousand impatiens in pink, orange, crimson, violet, and lilac. At the far end of the portico was a two-story apartment of some kind, made of the same brick and in the same design as the chateau, but quite separate from the main building, its door opening onto the portico, its windows overlooking the circular drive and the fountain on one side, a garden on the other. I was wondering if that was where the owners lived, when there was the slam of a car door from somewhere beyond the garden, and a familiar figure in sky-blue turtleneck and well-cut slacks appeared from behind some bushes and came toward me. My imaginary encounter come true: Here I was, face to face with Jan Sorrel in my terrycloth robe and rubber thongs.

He barely noticed me. A preoccupied nod and a twitch of a smile, and he disappeared inside the private apartment. I should have known there'd have to be some special arrangements for celebrity guests. One could hardly expect Bernstein, for instance, to have to listen to some businessman from New Jersey gargling next door.

I was curious about the slam of the car door. My Honda was no longer in the drive and I thought it would be nice to know where the beard had stowed it. I retraced Sorrel's path from the portico down across the edge of the garden and through the bushes. There, indeed, stood a row of parked cars, including the Honda. But more than that—far more than that—some thirty yards beyond the cars, against the edge of a forest, stood an old, gray, octagonal, hundred-foot tower.

Its wooden shingles had once been painted, to judge from the pale yellow streaks here and there, but had weathered to a dull silver. Four cracked stone steps led up to a weather-beaten door, and above the door, at intervals of twenty feet, one above the other, were two windows not more than two feet high and six or eight inches wide. Just below the second window was what looked like an octagonal clock, except that where the six would ordinarily be, there was the number fifteen. Above all this, some eighty feet in the air, was a railed balcony that encircled the tower and from which another door led to the interior. This door was ajar, and a bird flew out through it and perched on the railing. Above the bird the tower continued, in what looked like louvered panels, another twenty feet to a whimsical cupola topped by a very old weather vane.

It was the stuff of legends and fairy tales. I wouldn't have been surprised to learn that Charlotte Bronte's mad Mrs. Rochester had once inhabited it, or Mary Queen of Scots. It was irresistible. I crossed the grassy lot, went up the broken steps, and put my hand on the knob of the door. There was a padlock attached, but it was hanging loose, and the door, in fact, was standing a few inches open. I pushed, and the door opened onto a dark, hollow shaft reaching up, it seemed, forever. There was a smell of dust and damp and animals. I went cautiously forward and seemed to be walking on pebbles. Looking down, I realized that the floor was encrusted with ossified bird droppings.

I peered into the gloom and made out an assortment of odd articles standing and lying about in the corners. An old cot bed, a gilded bird cage, a child's stuffed toy, a golden goblet, an ancient icebox, pieces of foam rubber, a tangle of electrical wires. At one side there was a wooden staircase going up—into what? I turned, and something disgusting brushed my face—a cobweb. At that moment there was a sound behind me—a floorboard creaked under the weight of a human foot—and I froze.

Reason should have told me that I was a half-minute's run from a sunny and highly civilized hotel, but reason has no powers in the dark interior of a cobwebbed tower. Besides, my feet seemed to have glued themselves to the encrusted floor. I held my breath.

Then a gentle male voice said, "Quite a mess, isn't it?" and I turned again and saw a large but ordinary man standing there with a kindly smile and a fringe of sandy-gray hair surrounding a tanned dome.

Nevertheless I moved closer to the door as I said, "What is it all about? All these strange things—like somebody's attic."

"It was originally a water tower," he said. He opened the door wide and I slipped outside. "And then at some point there was a playhouse nearby and the actors stored their scenery and props in here." He closed the door carefully, fitted the padlock into place, and came down the broken steps in my wake. "They keep it locked, but they'll give you the key if you're curious and have the courage to explore it. It's quite a climb to the balcony." He gestured with the flashlight he was carrying and his intelligent brown eyes, heavy lidded, deeply set, long lashed, looked amused.

I looked up and shuddered at the thought of mounting the narrow gritty staircase in the dark. He smiled, a warm but somewhat sad smile.

"That's the water gauge," he said, pointing to what I had thought was a clock. "Those numbers would indicate the water level in the tank, which is housed in that top section. It's dry now, of course." He looked thoughtfully at the tower for another moment, then turned his back on it. "You know they call this the poodle tower? The Countess is said to have buried her dogs around the base of it, but the markers are overgrown and hard to find. It's interesting," he went on as we crossed to the line of parked cars. "I don't know that it's true of the Countess, but so many people who have no regard or concern for human life are very good to their dogs. What worthy quality do dogs have that humans lack?"

I laughed, thinking of George. "They forgive everything."

"Ah!" He smiled. "Well, enjoy your swim," he said, and made his way to the portico. I continued down to the bottom of the garden, as the beard had directed. It was dotted with whitewashed stone benches and several pitted and lichened pieces of statuary in which cherubs were entangled with unicorns in what might or might not have been innocent play. The path ended at a wrought-iron gate and beyond the gate the ground sloped down to a sun-filled grassy hollow surrounded by trees. In the center of this was a forty-foot oval of cool, deep blue water. The grass grew to the edge of the pool, no concrete surround, no diving board, just a quiet pool in a green hollow where wood nymphs could frolic on a midsummer's day.

The nymphs currently disporting themselves, however, were of somewhat less than perfect beauty. They consisted of a middleaged man and woman stretched out on adjacent redwood chaises, their pink skin shiny with tanning lotion.

I opened the gate and went down the half-dozen steps cut into the downward slope. The lady in the chaise raised her head, looked at me over her white plastic noseguard, and lay down again. I deposited my towel and robe on one of the chairs, lowered myself into the pool, and swam lazily back and forth, feeling cool and buoyant under the blue sky, with leaves rustling overhead and an occasional bird twittering nearby.

The birds led to thoughts of the tower. Judging by the encrustation on the floor, birds must have been nesting in there for the last thirty years, probably flying in through that open door high up on the balcony, left unlocked, I supposed, for air to circulate, since the miniscule windows were glassed in.

I turned over on my back and floated. If the boys and Elliot could only see me now! A twinge of guilt at the thought of Alan and Matt and their sweaty Beef and Brew jobs. To escape the guilt I returned mentally to the tower and wondered about the large, gentle man who'd been in there, and whether his curiosity had been piqued by the same associations that had occurred to me. I wondered how many other guests were staying at Wheatleigh and who they were. I wondered about Eleanor Springer and her daughter, and if they had finally gotten to wherever they were going.

After about twenty minutes I climbed out of the pool and began to towel my hair. The man in the chaise next to the lady with the plastic noseguard was sitting up, watching me.

"Hi!" he said heartily, giving me what can best be described as the glad eye. "How's the water?"

This is a question to which I have never been able to formulate an adequate reply.

"Lovely," I said.

The lady next to him sat up quickly and said, "Let's go back to the room. I want to take a shower."

There was a clank of the wrought-iron gate as someone opened it. I looked up. Two very decorative, long-legged females in bikinis with shirts over them were coming down the slope.

Eleanor and Jenny Springer.

4

AT A quarter to six we were following Shura Charnov's written directions out of Lenox, Greenfield beside me in a fresh shirt and gray slacks, his face slightly tanned from sitting on his private balcony reading William Manchester's *The Glory and the Dream*.

"As long as we're out," he said, "I heard of a good restaurant we might go to for dinner."

"But you already made a reservation at Wheatleigh."

"That was before those people arrived. Besides, it doesn't constitute an absolute obligation."

"Charlie," I said, "you can't spend all your time here thinking up ways to avoid Eleanor Springer. If you like, I'll tell her, in confidence, that you're a devout homosexual. I guarantee she won't come near you."

"I could," he said, "sedate you with Valium, drive you up to Monument Mountain at midnight, and leave you there."

"Or, I'll tell her you're a convicted rapist."

"That might not necessarily be a deterrent."

"Or, that you have a communicable disease. Don't worry, I'll think of something."

"I wish I could disbelieve you. We turn left here."

"No we don't."

"Maggie. We turn left."

"That's not what the directions say."

"Stop the car."

In spite of the directions, in spite of the fact that

Greenfield had been there several times, we managed to get lost. Somewhere I had taken the wrong turning, gone several miles out of the way, and, as we subsequently learned, approached the house from the wrong end of the road.

As a residential district it was somewhat heterogeneous; inexpensive frame houses built in the thirties and forties with economy more than beauty in mind stood on small plots that occasionally bordered an acre of lawn surrounding some boldly contemporary dwelling, while faded farmhouse adjoined rustic summer cottage, which abutted on conventional aluminum-sided ranch house—apparently it had experienced continual turnover in both land and property. Coming into it, unknowingly, from the wrong end of the road, the "fourth house on the right" proved to be the rather neglected-looking home of several small, happily grubby children playing out front, who had never heard of Charnov, which was a name they seemed to find hilarious.

One of them screamed for her mother and a hollow-chested young woman with an eager smile came out and asked if she could help. Apparently she couldn't, as she had only last week moved into the neighborhood. We left her shepherding her brood indoors and proceeded up the road, hoping Greenfield would eventually recognize a house. Shura had neglected to give us a number.

We came upon a tall, very skinny, very sour old man with very small eyes, watering a scruffy lawn with a hose in the company of a mangy-looking dog, and I pulled in to the curb. The dog began to bark hysterically and the man glared at us. Greenfield asked him if he happened to know the Charnovs.

"I don't get social," the man said in a down-East voice. "I mind my own business and stay in my own house. Let them stay in theirs."

Greenfield eyed the man for a moment and decided his need to know was greater than his need to squash. "The man we're looking for is a musician—"

"I pay my taxes and I'm entitled to my privacy."

"—about my age, with a small beard—"

"If a man can't have peace and quiet at the end of his life, when *can* he have it!"

"Immediately after the end of his life," Greenfield said, "is precisely when he can have it." He waved me on.

Two houses farther on, Greenfield said, "This is it." Fortunately it was, since Greenfield took the liberty of ignoring the front door of the cottage and walking around to the backyard, from which he could hear voices and where, I saw when I followed him, there were flowers and vegetables growing in gay abandon next to a brick patio on which Nadia Charnov had set out an array of things to nibble and a tray of bottles and glasses.

Nadia was a small, elegant woman with jet-black hair parted in the middle and pulled back into a ballerina's knot. She had quick brown eyes that missed nothing, high cheekbones, a pointed chin, and that easy assumption of being persona grata usually associated with those born to privilege. In Nadia's case the status was musical; she came from a family of well-known musicians and in her younger days had been a successful concert singer, so she moved in Tanglewood circles like a small duchess and took no guff from anybody.

She disposed quickly of the amenities as she plied us with drinks and avocado dip and sticks of Jerusalem artichoke.

"So, Charlie, how is your family, your girls? Karen is teaching? Very good. And Julie? The Grand Tetons, that's where? Ah! Must be beautiful. And Debbie? *Two* children now, that is marvelous. Our boys do very well. Richard now has a baby girl, he is a resident at Mass General. Vladi lives with a lady painter—talented? Who knows—they live in Greenwich Village and must always have the exterminator, and Vladi writes the score for a musical comedy, also a cantata for Lincoln Center. Please, Maggie, taste the cheese here—it's Fougerous, from France—they make it on the farms, not in factories—you see the vine leaf on top? That's how you tell Fougerous. So what do you think, Charlie, about this nonsense of Shura's? The balcony that collapsed and all the rest. It's ridiculous if you ask me."

"To Nadia," Shura said, as he poured white wine into a juice glass, "everything is ridiculous unless it has to do with food or Schubert. It was not a balcony. A *deck—*"

"Given the professional standards of most builders to-day—" Greenfield said.

"But Batista built it *himself,*" Shura said. "It's his hobby, building. And he claims there was evidence somebody cut through one of the supports."

"Batista!" Nadia disposed of him with a flick of the cheese parer.

"Noll looked at it. Noll agrees with him."

"Noel agrees with everybody. Have you met our neighbor?" she asked Greenfield, who nodded. "A curious man. He's only with the Symphony since—how long is it, Shura? Not even a year."

"Eight months. He replaced Warren Parry. Poor Warren got very sick with his ulcers."

"Not surprising," Greenfield said dryly, "it can't be easy for a simple Anglo-Saxon in that group."

Nadia lifted her pointed chin and bestowed a seraphic smile on Greenfield. "You are so clever, Charlie. That's one problem Damaskin will not have."

"What do you mean, 'one problem'?" Shura said. "Does he have *any?* Not that I can see."

"That's jealousy speaking. Shura is green with envy because of the Guarnerius." Nadia pursed her lips in a knowing way.

Greenfield was impressed. "He owns a Guarnerius?"

"A del Gesù! 1740! How much of it he owns, I don't know. He must have a mortgage on it for at least a hundred thousand."

"Have you heard it?"

Shura lifted a hand to express the inexpressible. "Sweet, like an Amati, but deep, rich, powerful!"

"No wonder he doesn't leave it in the locker," I said.

"In the *where?*"

"He was carrying his case when we met him."

"No, no." Shura smiled at my innocence. "That was his

practice violin. A Guarnerius you don't schlepp to rehearsals."

"So now," Nadia said, biting delicately on a cracker, "Shura will not rest until he has an Amati cello."

As I dipped a piece of artichoke into the avocado cream there was a faint "hello" and through the trees that separated the Charnovs' property from their neighbors' came Noel Damaskin, tanned and smiling and all but edible in a beige linen shirt and white corduroys.

He greeted us warmly, gave Nadia a kiss on the cheek and said, "You look gorgeous! That color is terrific on you." He appealed to us. "Isn't that color terrific on her?" He gave her another kiss and asked to borrow a bottle of vodka.

Nadia, who was striking in any color, including the current apricot, looked as though she had sprinkled the compliment liberally with salt before digesting it. She went off to get the vodka, and Noel seated himself comfortably in a garden chair.

"These people," he told us, "are perfect neighbors. They're never out of anything and they never complain about my practicing."

"Avery is still giving you trouble?" Shura asked.

"You wouldn't believe it. Two hours ago I was listening to Sorrel's recording of the Ravel—and sure enough he started that dog of his barking right under my window. He's trained the dog to bark on cue, and once it starts it can go on for an hour."

"I heard it," Shura said.

"This Avery," I asked, "is he a tall skinny man who looks as though he's been living on a diet of sour grapes?"

Shura nodded and Noel said, "You've met him!"

"Briefly," Greenfield said, "and bitterly."

Shura said, "He's a very cranky man."

Nadia, returning with the vodka, chimed in. "Who are you talking about? Avery? Of course, Avery. Some of these people, you know, who have lived here for years, maybe go back for generations, who knows—they really hate us. They hate musicians, they hate Tanglewood, they squeeze every

cent they can out of us—you should see what it costs to have
a plumbing leak fixed, or the television . . ."

"It's typical provincial mentality," Noel shrugged. "What
they don't understand, they hate. Bach, Beethoven . . . to
them it's like little men from Mars. We're an invasion."

"Not all of them," Shura protested. "The people at the
drugstore and the grocery are very friendly."

"Oh, yes," Nadia said, "many of them are very decent.
You always find good ones in the barrel."

"Frankly," Noel said, "I think Avery's a little off the
beam. He's been living alone in that house next to mine for
years, with no company but the dog . . ."

A faintly querulous voice came wafting through the trees.
"Noellll?"

"I'll be right there!" Noel called, and then to us, smiling
and showing no intention of bestirring himself, "I think next
year I'll have to build a house, farther out. I couldn't take
another summer of Avery."

A large, stately woman with a formidable bosom appeared, dressed in a blue silk caftan that billowed around
her as she sailed across the intervening space like the *Queen
Elizabeth II* coming into port. She was introduced to us as
Noel's wife. She looked several years older than her husband, had a rather plain face, a beauty-parlor hairdo, and a
matronly manner. She slipped her arm over Noel's shoulder,
achieved a half-smile, and began to pick nonexistent lint
from his shirt.

"I had a feeling you wouldn't be back," she said mildly.
"When musicians get together, a mere wife is easily forgotten. If only I'd been born with talent."

It was altogether too smooth to have been the first time
she'd said it.

"Talent!" Noel said, taking his cue, "I'd trade six fiddle
players for your boeuf en daube! Do you know," he demanded, "that this woman graduated summa cum laude
from the Cordon Bleu?"

"She is a superb cook," Nadia agreed. "She puts me to
shame. Fran, you must meet our friends—"

She introduced us, and Noel continued to make a display of husbandly pride so persistent and superfluous that I couldn't help wondering what was behind it. Since the Damaskins showed no signs of leaving, Nadia got busy making them vodka drinks out of an already opened bottle. I noticed, however, that they still took their borrowed bottle with them when they finally got up to go, which they did only when Nadia firmly announced that they would all be late for their dinner party if they didn't start out soon. Apparently the Damaskins and Charnovs had been invited to the same house, because Noel turned back as he and his wife were crossing the stretch to their own property and said, "Oh, Shura, a favor if you don't mind—I'm coaching a student chamber group later this evening—if I don't get back to the Prestons' in time, you'll take Fran home for me?"

"Of course," Shura said.

"Of course," Nadia repeated, once they were out of earshot. "And tomorrow it's your turn to drive again? Because poor Fran needs the car? How can you call this a car *pool* when he drives only once a week? And where is that garden shears you lent him last week? We'll never see it again."

Shura grinned. "So why did you give him the vodka?"

"For God's sake, Shura, I'm not a peasant. If you have it, you give it. Only there's a limit."

We left them with Nadia insisting that we come for dinner the following night.

"Tomorrow night," Greenfield said, "you'll be *my* guests."

"Nonsense," Nadia said. "Ridiculous. I have already bought everything. I am marinating the veal. If it's not Cordon Bleu you won't mind." Her dark eyes twinkled wickedly.

By convincing Greenfield that without having made an advance reservation we would be in for a long wait at any other decent eating place, I persuaded him to risk Eleanor Springer and return to Wheatleigh. As it happened, she was not there, nor was Jenny. We dined comfortably in the main dining room, a glowing Victorian room, all crimson and white, a single perfect rose in a slender vase on each table, with an assortment of other guests for company.

There was a voluble quartet of young marrieds at one table discussing backhands, bungled serves, and playing the net. If the tennis roster on the elegant bulletin board was accurate, they were either the Polks and the Sturmans, nine to ten, or the Gornicks and the Halpers, ten to eleven.

At another table a very old man with skin like pale pink crepe paper, and two old women, one resembling a wren in eyeglasses, the other an eagle in what looked like a bed jacket trimmed in dim maribou, were silently sipping wine and occasionally taking a bite of food.

Directly opposite our table, the large, gentle man from the tower sat alone, reading from a book at the side of his plate, so completely absorbed that it wasn't until the waitress came to clear away and ask about dessert that he looked up. Noticing me, he smiled, and I smiled back, whereupon Greenfield raised an inquiring eyebrow and I told him that was the man I'd mentioned meeting in the tower.

Greenfield was always curious about men who read books while dining alone, ever since he'd struck up an acquaintance with an archeologist in a dining car, on a train in Mexico, who was leafing through a book about a dig in the Yucatan. Greenfield now had a groundless conviction that any such man must have fascinating interests. I wasn't too surprised when, the large man having finished his lemon mousse and closed his book, Greenfield asked if he would care to join us for a second cup of coffee.

The man accepted, drew up a chair, and told us his name was Isadore Mirisch. The book, as a clue to an exotic profession, was indeterminate. Greenfield, glancing at the title of the volume he'd brought with him, said aloud in a hollow tone, "The Plays of Shakespeare!"

Isadore Mirisch smiled at the implied question and said, "It was sitting on my night table when I was packing and I dropped it in my suitcase."

Not on anything breakable, I trusted. It was a hefty book.

"I thought perhaps you were doing research," Greenfield said with a certain melancholy. "But I don't imagine the Elizabethan period needs any more researching. You're not a scientist by any chance?"

Mirisch shook his head. "I work for a publishing firm," he said, "in Boston." He stirred his sugarless coffee and asked Greenfield what his work was, and before long the conversation turned, as it invariably did in the immediate neighborhood, to Tanglewood, and the upcoming concert, and music in general. When Greenfield confessed that he trifled with a cello in his spare time, there was a quickening of interest in Mirisch's eyes. Then he looked down at his coffee and said, "When I was a child, I wanted very badly to be in the school band and they needed a trumpet, so I studied the trumpet for a few months." He laughed softly. "I just wasn't meant to play the trumpet. At my lessons the teacher would invariably get annoyed and say, 'If Judgment Day depended on you, nobody would ever be called to account for anything.' I never made the band." He discarded the subject with a gesture. "A millennium ago."

I decided I liked Isadore Mirisch, and lifted my cup to sip at my coffee, when there was a sudden and alien sensation around my legs. I looked down and saw Nefertiti rubbing against them. Simultaneously, Jenny Springer appeared.

"Oh, there you are." She picked up the cat under one arm. She was wearing her dark glasses again and how she could see anything was a mystery. "She ran out of the room when I opened the door," she said, sitting down. "She gets restless at night. She has a very strong libido and practically no morals. I told her she probably wasn't going to find any male cats around here, but she's so weird she could probably be happy with a raccoon or a beaver or whatever's around. How was the dinner here? We went to an Italian restaurant. The waiters kept getting together in corners and whispering. I think it's a Mafia joint. You want some sugar, Nef?" She opened one of the small paper packets of sugar and held it under the cat's nose.

Isadore Mirisch looked bewildered. Greenfield looked

persecuted and motioned the waitress to bring the bill. I got
Jenny and the cat out of the dining room and into the hall
where I sank into a corner of the sofa, surfeited with food,
wine, and strangers. Jenny sat beside me, not yet surfeited
with any aspect of living.

"Where's your mother?" I asked, thinking I might suggest
she join her.

"I don't know. We came back about an hour ago and then
she decided she had to have some peaches. She said there
was a supermarket on the road to Pittsfield that stayed open
late. She never eats after dinner so there must be some
reason she took off."

"People sometimes like to be alone," I said, not without
point.

Greenfield and Isadore Mirisch came in from the dining
room and stood by a table in the corner looking down at a
chess board someone had left in mid-game. The tall arched
door at the front of the Hall opened, and the lady of the
plastic noseguard came in, followed by her husband.

"Jacob's Pillow," she was saying.

"Oh God, I really don't like modern dance."

"Well, we can't get tickets for the play, and we're going
to the concert Friday, what are we going to do tomorrow—
just sit around here all night?"

"I think I'd like some brandy." His glance crossed the sofa
and he stopped. "Hi there," he said to me, "care to join us
for a drink?"

The polite, prim smile on the wife's face went as stiff as
though she'd been flash-frozen. Oh, goodness gracious, did I
need this?

"No, thanks."

"You have dinner here?"

"Yes."

"We tried Village Inn. Just to see what it was like."

"Oh! There are the Harrises!" his wife said jauntily, and
took his arm in no uncertain terms. They went off to the bar,
which was formerly the library and still lined with books,
and which opened off the Hall at the far end.

"Last year," Jenny said, apropos of what she had obviously observed, "there was a man here with his wife and he kept hanging around Rita, the girl who worked in the bar, until he found out she's married to a construction worker who comes to pick her up every night after work, who's six foot seven. He used to work in a circus, Rita's husband, I mean, and they traveled all over the world. Once they went to South America and he got drunk and the circus left without him and he was stranded in the mountains of Bolivia."

"What are you studying in college?" I asked.

"Film," she said.

"Good." When I said it, she looked up, sensing irony.

The front door opened again to admit Eleanor Springer, in a diaphanous white shirt and flowered skirt and a slightly red nose. The expressionlessness of her face had somehow deepened.

"It's getting a little cooler," she said listlessly. And then, to Jenny, "I'm going to bed."

Jenny squinted up at her. "It's only nine thirty."

"I'm tired. Do you have your key?"

"I can get one in the office. Anybody can get one. They're just hanging there. Anyone could walk in and take a key to any room. We could be asleep in our beds in the middle of the night and the door could open—"

"Oh, don't do that," Eleanor said wearily, and dropped some damp, crumpled tissue in the ashtray on the coffee table. "Besides, it isn't true."

"Where are the peaches?" Jenny asked.

Eleanor hesitated. "They weren't very good," she said finally. "Small and hard. I didn't get any." She gave a hint of a tired smile. "Goodnight."

She crossed to the staircase and went up.

"My mother," Jenny said, "is manic-depressive. And very boring." So far I had seen no evidence of the manic. Nefertiti jumped into my lap. I handed her back to Jenny. "Why don't you take her out to look at the moon," I suggested. "It's not good to be entirely cut off from your past." I stood up. My little room and my Graham Greene were beckoning.

I said goodnight to Jenny, and Greenfield, and Isadore Mirisch, and went upstairs.

In the blue-and-white room it was peaceful and private, one small lamp making a warm glow on the white curtains at the casement windows. I went close to the window screens to see if I could see a moon, and made a discovery.

The windows overlooked a side patch of lawn, a piece of graveled drive, and the service entrance, and just at that moment the dining room waitresses began to depart down below, the service door opening and closing with a bang each time one or two of them came through. There would be a brief interval of giggling, complaining, or teasing, then a car would start up noisily and screech off down the drive. I sighed for my lost quiet and prepared for bed, but eventually they were all gone and peace returned. I opened *The Honorary Consul.*

It wasn't until my eyes, which had been open since six thirty that morning, began closing over the book, and I put out the light, that I heard voices again. There were a man's and a woman's, and they were low and intense. I tried to ignore them, but they went on and on, and the fact that they were audible without being intelligible proved too provocative. I got out of bed. Either I would tell them they were keeping me awake, or I would well and truly eavesdrop; a middle course was beyond my patience.

I bent to the screen and saw the flicker of a flashlight being played over the lawn, and a man and a woman with their heads down, searching.

"Maybe it wasn't here you lost it, Jan," the woman said, in thin, accented tones.

"Yes, yes, when we were taking that walk. Because I had it in my hand when we left the room, and when we reached the back lawn there, I thought to put it in my pocket, and I didn't have it."

I recognized the voice. And the cap of gold hair. It was Sorrel. And madam, obviously.

"Well," she said, "we can't stay looking all night. Wait until morning, we'll look again."

"I hate to lose things!" Sorrel hissed. "On top of everything. All this trouble. Nothing but trouble here. How could someone spill ink on the oboe part? How could that happen? They can't possibly copy it out in time. There's no extra part. He will have to play from the score! The librarian will have to sit beside him and keep a finger on the part! Inexcusable!" His voice trailed off as they moved toward the front of the house.

I went back to bed and lay there staring at the pale square of the window where oblique light from the moon touched the curtains. My mind toyed with what it was Sorrel had lost: a key? a wallet? a bottle of hair dye? From these idle speculations I drifted to thoughts of Eleanor Springer, going out to buy peaches and coming back with nothing but a wad of Kleenex that was damp from being cried into. I somehow doubted that the frustration of not being able to find good peaches was sufficient cause for weeping. "Frustration" brought me back to Sorrel and ink on the oboe part, and from there to a bassoonist's cantilevered deck collapsing, and a flutist being forced off the road, and a second violinist receiving a strange letter.

Was it possible? Did someone have it in for the BSO?

I decided it wasn't possible, because I was on vacation and everything was supposed to be just lovely, and I fell asleep.

5

"WILL YOU be ready," Greenfield asked from behind his newspaper the following morning, "to leave for rehearsal at nine forty-five?"

We were sitting on the terrace after breakfast. It was the kind of terrace they used to have in those Cary Grant movies: an opulent stretch of grass squares separated by graveled paths, ending on either side in porticos supported by Roman columns entwined with luxuriant dark green vines that trailed on the tiled portico floors, a knee-high balustrade banked with a riot of flowers running along the front of the terrace to a set of wide, shallow stone stairs leading down to several acres of lawn, and a view, across the lawn and the forest beyond it, of a lake ringed with mountains.

We sat in a vast, morning quiet, still and hushed, the sky a pale blue backdrop for the coppery green trees, a single streamer of white cloud unmoving above a mountain top, not a sound from anywhere, the air so still even the grass seemed to have stopped growing. I stretched in the sun. A jackrabbit ran silently across the lawn and disappeared.

I said, in answer to Greenfield's question, "Think you can walk it in ten minutes?"

He looked up. "Why?" he said. "What happened to the car?"

It was not that Greenfield was averse to exercise, it was just that it never occurred to him as a viable way of life, given the number of more important things on his mind.

"Nothing," I said, "I thought walking might be a good idea after all that French toast."

He frowned, faced with an unexpected revision in his timetable.

Through the doors opening from the Hall, the man with the glad eye and his apprehensive wife came onto the terrace.

"How about Chesterwood?" she was asking him.

"What's that?"

"The man who sculpted the statue of Lincoln for the memorial in Washington. It's his studio. It's just outside of Stockbridge."

"What can you see there?"

"Well—it's his *studio*."

"All right, all right. Sure." He sounded as enthusiastic as a ten-year-old invited to a meeting of the Ladies' Choral Society.

As they passed, he stopped to beam down at me and deliver his favorite greeting. "Hi, there!"

I mumbled, "Morning."

The wife forced her rigid lips to curve upward.

"Lovely morning," he continued.

"We're going to Chesterwood," she said, and dragged him off.

Greenfield looked at me with a hint of disapproval. "Do you *know* that man?"

"You mean in the Biblical sense?"

Despairing of me, he folded his paper and stood up. I relented and said, "I don't even know his name."

"I heard someone call him Felker. He doesn't strike me as an intellectual giant. If we're going to *walk*," he said, as though speaking of a cross-country trek, "we'd better start at nine thirty."

We did. The road was deserted and the air was still fresh and smelled of summer morning. I told Greenfield, as we walked, about my discovery the night before of Sorrel beneath my window, and the incident of the ink on the oboe part. He stopped by the side of the road, stared ahead thoughtfully at Hawthorne's little red house for a while, made no comment, and continued walking.

"Does that mean you think there's a plot?" I asked. "Or you think there's a pebble in your shoe?"

"There's a strange consistency in these incidents," he said, "assuming we have any reason to consider them the work of one person. At this point they could just as easily be a series of unrelated phenomena."

I didn't see any consistency in them, but before I could pursue the subject, he changed it.

"Consider this place in the mid-eighties," he said, "Hawthorne sitting in that house shivering through the winter writing *The House of the Seven Gables,* Melville living at Arrowhead up the road, writing *Moby Dick,* Longfellow and Oliver Wendell Holmes in the vicinity—I don't know what they were writing, but it certainly wasn't something called *Airport.*"

"Maybe it was easier to have integrity in the mid-eighties."

"Rubbish. Melville was in agony because he couldn't make a dollar with the things he wanted to write, and couldn't write the stuff that did make money, and finally had to settle for something in between. The battle between the artist and his stomach goes back to the first hungry boy with a sharp stone who had to draw some banality on the wall of the head man's cave before he got his piece of dinosaur meat. The difference between Melville and a hack is the difference between intelligent compromise and venality."

> "'Alas, 'tis true, I have gone here and there,
> And made myself a motley to the view,
> Gored mine own thoughts, sold cheap what is
> most dear—'"

Greenfield stopped and looked at me as though I'd just sprouted green hair. "You also travel with Shakespeare in your suitcase?"

"No," I waved a hand airily, "just happened to remember

it. That's odd, isn't it, about Mirisch. You don't find anyone but an off-Broadway actor reading Shakespeare these days."

"Or a scholar. Mirisch is neither."

"What is he, then?"

"At a guess—a displaced nineteenth-century cabinet maker."

I thought about this.

"Not venal," I concluded.

"Far from venal. The polar opposite."

We went in through the Lion's Gate, and I looked at my watch.

"Seventeen minutes," I announced. "Not bad."

Greenfield began to cut across the lawn toward the Music Shed. The thought of being confined once more under a roof did not appeal to me.

I said, "You go ahead. I'm going to sit on the lawn."

He raised an eyebrow, but went off without a word, and I wandered along the path toward the Main House. It was a rambling, hundred-year-old building painted dark green, with a deep porch encircling it, which held offices and practice rooms. You could sit on that porch and see for miles, across the acres of lawn, over the ten-foot-high hedge of Canadian hemlock enclosing the Tanglewood grounds, all the way to the waters of the Stockbridge Bowl and the far mountains.

The sound of a student quartet playing Mozart drifted down from a third-story window, and I thought of those Friday night sessions at Gordon Oliver's, with Greenfield saying, "If you want to play *ensemble*, it's not enough to *count*, you have to *listen*." According to Greenfield, it was always my piano or Gordon's violin that was a beat, or a bar, or sometimes a half-page too early or too late; never his cello.

It was still a few minutes short of the start of rehearsal, and I went up on the porch and scanned the large bulletin boards, which posted separate schedules for Vocalists, Instrumentalists, Composers, Conductors, and one, evidently, for general use.

The "general" bulletin board was a mine of miscellaneous announcements.

"Hungry? Come learn about edible plants."

My God, I thought, are they starving the musicians?

"Anyone interested in duets, trios, etc., with pianist, please contact Melanie Belsen, 8176."

"The fee for replacing a B.M.C. membership card is $35."

"Bassoon instruction wanted—"

"First permanent bus schedule"

"Viola for sale—"

"If you want to share expenses and driving to N.Y.—"

And one rather cryptic message from one student to another that made me smile, imagining some promising young composer arranging his tryst with a budding flutist in some sylvan glade, "N. Same time same place. A."

From the Music Shed there were isolated sounds of instruments being tuned. I went down to the lawn and sat under an ancient fir, its patriarchal roots surfacing for yards around the base, its huge, gnarled lower limbs trailing on the ground. By now there was considerable cacophony from the Shed: conflicting shrieks, wails, honks, and pipings, like a flock of agitated gulls wheeling raucously over the sea.

This went on for some time, various instruments practicing a difficult passage here or there. Eventually most of the instruments fell quiet. Then, after a pause, another isolated trial flight from a horn, a cello, an oboe—they were certainly taking their time getting started.

Finally, total silence. Then—

Ravel.

The hushed, mysterious repetition of four notes. The opening of the *Rapsodie Espagnole*. A sudden crescendo, with the force of a huge breaker gathering height and washing onto the beach. Again the hushed, hypnotic notes. The music washed over the grass, over the trees, over the Main House and the fields beyond, over the Stockbridge Bowl and the mountains, lifting New England into the sky and setting it down in Spain. Sensuous, seductive, the teasing Andalusian rhythms evoked the harsher sunlight, the ochre walls, the red rose in the black hair, the proud tilt of the head over sinuous shoulder, the calculating, smouldering, sidelong glance, and all the rich color, all the flamboyance, all the austere and dangerous passion of Goya's land.

And into this Spanish courtyard walked Eleanor Springer, crossing my vision a hundred yards away, not seeing me, staring straight ahead, moving languorously but in a straight line toward the source of the music. She wore white pants and a loose, silky, amethyst-colored shirt, but she might have been dressed in clinging black with a cascade of ruffles falling from her hips, so completely did she embody the music.

I wouldn't have been surprised if she'd continued, in her trance, straight into the Shed and up the aisle onto the platform and ravished Jan Sorrel in front of everybody.

Apparently she didn't, as the music continued unbroken long after I'd lost sight of her.

At intermission I wandered over to the Shed to find Greenfield. He was no longer there, but Eleanor was, sitting in the first row with her eyes staring at an empty stage. I went around to the backstage area, thinking Greenfield had probably gone to debate with Shura the fine points in the difference between Sorrel's interpretation and Von Karajan's. I couldn't see him, or Shura, but all the other musicians seemed to be there, exchanging stories, discussing solar heating, and milling around a coffee urn presided over by a teenage boy and set up on a table with paper cups, dishes of chocolate brownies and cream-cheese-filled bagels, and a sign explaining that these goodies were meant for the sole consumption of the orchestra personnel.

I passed by Noel Damaskin, coffee in one hand, bagel in the other, proclaiming to a group of three, "This is good. This is what life is all about. Is there any substitute for a bagel? Nothing is like a bagel. Not even a fast car. Or a virgin."

There was light laughter. For some reason there always is

when the word *virgin* is spoken, the way there is at *odds
bodkins* or other archaic expressions.

I saw Greenfield, finally, coming around the far end of the
building with Shura, and then a voice over a PA system
suggested it was time for the musicians to resume their
chores, and I went to sit in the Shed with Greenfield for the
second half of rehearsal. The sun was beating down and the
temperature was rising. The musicians drifted onstage, one
man holding his T-shirt away from his chest with two
fingers to cool himself, another taking a violin from a group
of three that had been deposited, for the break, on top of a
gray-painted organ near the entrance, then putting it back
and taking another instead, wiping it off tenderly with his
handkerchief. How did he know, I wondered, which violin
was his, when to me they all looked identical?

I surveyed the audience. Eleanor was sitting in the first
row and I glanced at her several times, wondering whether
her face would finally be forced to express what she was
feeling, in the immediacy of Sorrel's presence. But whenever
I looked, she seemed to be staring at the first violins. I concluded that either Prokofiev's ballet score for *Romeo and
Juliet* did not allow Sorrel's charisma full reign, or the angle
from which I was observing her was giving me a false im-
pression. I concentrated on *Romeo and Juliet,* marveling yet
again that the words of one inspired Englishman had per-
vaded so many aspects of life for so many hundreds of years.
Suddenly it was 12:30 and the musicians were leaving, and
Greenfield was standing.

"I've arranged a lift back to Wheatleigh," he said. "For
you as well, if you like."

"After all this sitting? No thanks, I'll walk."

"Mad dogs and Englishmen," he murmured, and went off
in the direction of the musicians' exit.

Eleanor had gone, but as I left the Shed I noticed the
three elderly people from Wheatleigh sitting on one of the
side benches. The two old ladies were keeping the sun off
their heads with straw mandarin hats tied under their frail
chins. The old man wore a yellow golf cap.

"I don't know why," the eagle was saying with disapproval, "they play so much of this *modern* music."

"In London," the wren piped up, "on any weekend—*any weekend*—you can hear the *1812 Overture*."

"Perhaps." The eagle was not soothed. "But even there, on the South Bank, they allow those *hordes* of children to go skate-boarding right by the concert halls!"

As I passed them I gave them a smile, and the old man smiled back, the wren looked uncertain, and the eagle cast a jaundiced eye in my direction.

I went to the cafeteria, ate a sandwich and drank a container of milk, then took off my sandals and started out barefoot across the lawn toward the Lion's Gate. Grass on bare feet, leaves moving in a hot breeze, air pungent with earth smells, sun bronzing my arms and legs, and the voluptuous strains of the Ravel returning to haunt me, I almost fell over Isadore Mirisch before I saw him. He was sitting in the green shade of a giant hickory, a picnic lunch spread on the ground before him, his large back bent over a dish of fruit and cheese and a carafe of white wine.

"Ah!" he said, smiling with his soft, heavy-lidded eyes, "bare feet. What a good idea. Brings you closer to the music."

"Then why are you wearing shoes?"

He shrugged. "After a certain age these things don't occur to you. What did you think of the Ravel? You looked transported."

I sat on the grass beside him. "I didn't see you, so I must have been. I'm afraid I didn't *think* anything about it. With Ravel I just swoon. Ravel *and* Tanglewood. What a combination."

"Yes," he said softly, and gazed across the lawn with a sudden look of anguish. "I wonder how long they'll let us keep it."

My heart lurched. "What do you mean?"

He smiled again. "No mass appeal. Ergo no profit. Ergo no use. The current World Credo." He sliced a piece of the

Gouda with an ivory-handled penknife and held it out to me.

"No, thanks, I've just had a sandwich."

"Some fruit? Some wine?"

I shook my head. "What kind of things does your firm publish? I only ask because Charlie's thinking of doing a book—he doesn't think I know but I do—about the early days of television newscasting. I thought it would be nice if he had a friend in high places."

Mirisch swallowed his cheese and smiled gently. "I wouldn't be any use to him. I'm hardly in high places and I handle textbooks, mainly. Have you ever heard Leinsdorf conduct the Prokofiev? A much different interpretation. A sharper focus. Somehow the strings . . . scintillated under Leinsdorf."

Which put me in my place quite neatly. No personal questions, thank you. A very private man.

We discussed the Prokofiev briefly and I stood up. "That sun," I said, "is really throwing its weight around. I've got to get back and swim."

He looked up at me with his sweet, quiet smile and said, "It's been nice talking with you."

By the time I got back and up to my room, I was a great deal hotter. I changed quickly and took my new route to the pool. I'd finally discovered an alternative to descending the Grand Staircase and crossing the Hall in my bathing attire; by crossing the second-floor gallery to the opposite wing and continuing on past Eleanor and Jenny Springer's room, I could get down by a staircase that debouched at the door to the front portico, just across the ground-floor corridor from Greenfield's room. Jenny had told me about it at the pool the day before, and I'd found it, with a discreet sign at the foot of it, stating that resident guests only were permitted beyond this point.

I'd been looking forward to a solitary swim in my little green dell, but when I got there, the pool was considerably occupied, which annoyed me. I didn't mind Jenny, who was slithering from one end to the other and not taking up much room, but there was also Felker, lumbering back and forth across the middle, and his wife, thrashing ineffectually around the perimeter, keeping her hairdo well clear of the water. Arrayed in chaises at the far end, the tennis quartet was tanning itself and talking nonstop, and one or all of them might decide at any moment to take a dip. If that happened it would be like swimming in a punch bowl too full of fruit.

I decided to wait, and went back up the garden, taking the path to the rear of the chateau, which led to the terrace. There, in the long wicker chair, in the quiet of the shaded portico with its vine-covered columns and the flowers, the lawn, the lake, the mountains, spread out before him, the Roman emperor C. B. Greenfield was taking his ease, a long cool lemonade at his elbow, and William Manchester in his hand. He didn't even look up as I wandered past him and across the terrace, down the stone stairs and across the lawn to the far side of the building. I meandered on, striking out across the side lawn, which reached to the entrance road, and ending up at the tennis court, where, of all things, I saw Jan Sorrel sending a smashing serve across the net to Noel Damaskin.

A lady who could only have been Mrs. Sorrel sat on the sidelines, looking cool and distant. She was built like a Borzoi, svelte and slightly emaciated, and she was smoking a cigarette in a holder, watching the two bronzed men in their tennis whites competing like mad in the heat of the sun.

It made me hotter just to watch them and I decided I'd get into the pool, empty or full. Fortunately it was empty. The Felkers had departed, Jenny was stretched out on a chaise, and the tennis quartet had turned over onto its collective stomach. I did twenty laps before one of them joined me. I got out and waited for him to exhaust himself, then did another twenty, climbed out and sat down beside Jenny. It was the first time I'd seen her without her dark glasses, and her eyes were lovely, gray and almond-shaped.

"I saw your mother at the rehearsal. Why didn't you come?"

"I was helping Wendell set up a show. He works at the Emporium in Stockbridge. The gallery. Con-tem-po-ra-ry Crafts. He's all right. A little Strindbergian, but not bad."

"Do you know him from the city?"

"No, I met him this morning. I drove in with my mother. She had to get some new makeup so she could play tennis with Mr. Mirisch—"

"With Mr. *Mirisch?*"

"Why not, is he a terrific player? My mother can hardly play."

"I have no idea," I said, wondering why the news was such a jolt.

I closed my eyes while Jenny prattled on, and when I opened them again it was to see Sorrel and his wife and Damaskin coming down the slope to the pool.

"Somehow," Jenny said, "you never expect to see a symphony conductor in swimming trunks. Who's the other man?"

"A violinist with the orchestra."

"Really." She got up and jumped into the pool.

Sorrel and Damaskin were going through an animated review of their tennis game, with Damaskin apologizing, saying he couldn't understand what had happened, he seemed to be off his form today, and complimenting Sorrel extravagantly on his game. They took chairs next to us, but Damaskin was so busy watching Jenny glide around the pool he didn't notice me. Then they went into the pool and Jenny came out, saying "If I were a dolphin I'd never go into show business, I'd only leap for my own pleasure." She slipped a wrinkled shirt over her wet bikini. "I'm going to take some pictures of this place, maybe I can sell them to one of those magazines they read in Connecticut. Want to come?"

I declined. She went up the slope dangling her towel from her fingers, and I gave myself up to the sun, trying not to think about the terrible aging process that was doubtless taking place as I tanned away.

After a while Sorrel came out of the pool, looking refreshed, shaking the water from his golden hair. Damaskin followed, looking as though he'd been working hard. The polished tan of his face had lost its rosiness and his chest rose and fell visibly as he went to a chair for his towel. This time he noticed me, registered surprise, and gave me a greeting before joining the Sorrels in a discussion of some musical criticism in a copy of the *Times* Mrs. Sorrel was holding. I went back into the water, and when I emerged they were jointly doing the crossword puzzle, though it was Damaskin who held the paper and the pencil.

"Eighty-four Across," he was saying, "four letters. Palindrome for isle of exile. Isle of exile . . . Aha!" he said triumphantly, "Able!"

The Sorrels applauded, and they went on to consider Thirty-two Across, subtropical plant, and Seven Down, obsidian, for short. Finally Damaskin got up from the chair and said, "I'd better get back and change for rehearsal. It was a wonderful game—really appreciate it—and the swim—" With a gesture worthy of David Niven, he raised Mrs. Sorrel's long thin hand to his lips. "If you get to Boston this winter, let's have a game at the indoor courts and I'll try to redeem myself."

"I'd love to see Boston," Mrs. Sorrel said in her high, fluty voice.

Damaskin looked surprised. "Oh, you didn't go along last time?"

"Last time?" she said.

"I told you before," Sorrel said politely, "I flew in and out for a quick meeting. I saw the airport and Symphony Hall, and nothing else."

"I see, and you didn't join him." Damaskin treated Mrs. Sorrel to a portion of charm. "Boston's loss," he said. "Do you know he's got a double? I could have sworn I saw him on Boylston Street, coming out of . . . well!" He turned on the smile, picked up his towel, repeated his thanks and goodbyes, and went up to the wrought-iron gate and out.

As he opened the gate something tawny streaked through the gate and down to the pool. With a sudden lurch of fear that she would go over the side, I ran to get the cat, my bare

foot landing on something ridged and rubbery. The cat
went for it, but I scooped it up with one hand and her with
the other. The Sorrels were gathering up their things and
holding a rapid conversation in a language that could have
been Czech or Hungarian. They left as I wriggled into my
robe, transferring Nefertiti from one arm to the other,
picked up my tote bag and stuffed the towel into it, and the
damned cat wriggled out of my arms and landed on the
Times crossword Damaskin had left behind. I grabbed her
again, picked up the *Times* as well—you never know when
an unfinished crossword puzzle will come in handy—and
started up the slope. Jenny met me at the gate, holding a
complicated-looking camera, still wearing the wrinkled
shirt. She took the cat and we walked up the path.

"Did she slip out of the room again?" I asked.

"Out of the car, when I went to get my camera. My
mother has one of her famous headaches. She didn't want
Nef in the room. She wanted to lie down in 'peace and
quiet and oblivion.' So I let Nef run around and then I put
her in the car so I could go to the pool. She hates the car."

"I thought your mother had a tennis date," I said.

"Four thirty. Maybe that's what she's resting for. I'm
going to shoot those Tiffany windows, you sure you don't
want to watch me being a photographer?"

"I have an appointment," I said, "with a four-thirty rehearsal."

"God, do you go to *all* of them?"

"This is my last one. I leave in the morning."

Her face fell. "*Why?*"

"Because there's no justice in the world."

We separated as she went to the right toward the parking
place and I went up onto the front portico and through the
door leading to the back staircase.

Greenfield was approaching the door of his room, key in
hand.

"What's a palindrome?" I asked him.

He looked glumly at my wet hair. "It's a quarter to four,"
he said.

"I'll be ready. Here." I handed him the puzzle. "Whatever it is, Damaskin got it in five seconds. I'll be right down."

As he disappeared into his room I turned past the discreet sign forbidding non-residents to mount the stairs, only to find a non-resident descending them: Noel Damaskin. I might have wondered more about what he was doing there if I hadn't been wondering why he looked, suddenly, like the last person I would choose to spend an hour running around a tennis court returning Sorrel's slashing serves. He managed a smile and rushed out, and I went to my room and changed back into clothes.

On the way to Tanglewood Greenfield was still working on the puzzle, coming up with such tricky answers as praesidium, Boadicea, neap, and fulcrum. By the time we got there he had finished the whole thing.

When we took our seats in the Music Shed, the musicians were coming onstage one and two at a time, ambling, clomping, shuffling, one of them brisk and purposeful, one of the women depositing her neat straw handbag at her feet. All of them began to tune as soon as they were seated.

Sorrel came onstage with his vigorous stride, fussed with the score, murmured to the concertmaster, raised the baton, and the music began. Ravel? Again? He must be worried about it. Sorrel, in fact, seemed to be on edge. Nothing pleased him; there seemed to be more rapping of baton than playing of notes. He never raised his voice, but the tone indicated he would like to.

Tap, tap. "Before twelve, please. Three before twelve. Percussion, what happened to you back there?"

Tap, tap. "You are giving me a sound like a kitten, I want a sound like a tiger. Again, please."

Tap, tap. "I do not hear the low-register flute there. I would like to hear low-register flute. If you please."

Tap, tap. "Ritard, gentlemen. Ritard. Ritard. Now once again, from the trombones . . ."

Toward the end of the Ravel there was a slight disturbance among the first violins. If I hadn't been watching them at the moment, I'd never have noticed. It was only the tiniest momentary breaking of ranks, a slight turning of a head, a shoulder. Sorrel dropped his baton arm to his side and swung the other up in a stop signal. A soaring phrase trailed off.

"That is not a crescendo, gentlemen. You are pussy-footing."

One of the violinists got halfway up from his seat with his mouth open. It was Noel Damaskin. He stared at Sorrel and slowly subsided without saying anything. He looked quite pale.

The other musicians glanced at him curiously. Holchek, his pudgy sidekick, gave him a baleful look and turned back to the music. Damaskin said something to him. Holchek replied shortly. Damaskin leaned forward and made a note on his music. Sorrel looked down at his score. I looked at Greenfield. Greenfield glanced sideways at me and back at the stage. Sorrel tapped with his baton.

"I am not happy with the triplets. They should be like machine gun. *Da*-da-da, *Da*-da-da. From the triple forté, please."

He raised his arms and the music thundered out across the auditorium, and suddenly there was no one playing beside Holchek. Damaskin had crumpled and was sliding off the chair. Holchek jumped to his feet. The music broke off with a snap, like the limb of a tree. The small audience was on its feet. My mouth went dry. Sorrel stood frozen with his hands in the air. Greenfield stood and made for the aisle. Musicians were converging on Damaskin's stand. There were gasps and startled cries on the stage, in the auditorium. I pushed my way out to the aisle and followed Greenfield to the foot of the stage. Sorrel was holding his head with one hand, the baton arm limp at his side.

Two men came running on from the entrance at the right, another from the left. Holchek was shaking his bald dome vigorously. There were exclamations from all sides, fragments of questions:

". . . did you notice . . . ?"

". . . seemed all right . . ."
". . . what was he . . . ?"
". . . don't move him!"
". . . call a doctor?"
". . . but I thought he was . . ."
". . . coronary?"

Greenfield was watching the scene with an expression of wary curiosity. He turned from the stage, found an aisle clear of people and inched his way to the far side of the Shed, with me in his wake.

On the grass outside the entrance to the musicians' locker rooms, a small group of musicians was huddled together looking, according to temperament, uneasy, philosophical, or frightened. Only dour, implacable Holchek, with his paunch and his jowls and his wire glasses, came calmly out and stood by himself, filling a pipe.

In the locker room doorway Shura appeared, looking ashen. He came dazedly down the steps and Greenfield went up to him. He stared at Greenfield with a look of astonished incredulity.

"He's dead!" he whispered.

6

AT A little before eight we were on our way to the Charnovs'. Greenfield had suggested, in the light of recent events, that they forget the dinner invitation, but Shura and Nadia wouldn't hear of it.

I could think of more relaxing ways of spending my last evening in the Berkshires than dining within a stone's throw of the recently deceased musician's house, but I had a feeling Nadia wanted Shura to have company, and that was reason enough for me. So I'd have a little trouble swallowing.

"I seem to remember," I said to Greenfield as we drove out of Lenox after stopping to purchase a bottle of Chateau Margaux Pavillon Blanc, "some bard's trenchant remark about the funeral meats being barely cold—"

But Greenfield was not listening. He looked, staring straight ahead with his chin pushing his mouth into an inverted U, fully occupied. I thought I knew what was occupying him, and I put out a feeler.

"It didn't look like a heart attack to me," I said, trying again. "People having heart attacks always clutch their chests. Or at least indicate where the pain is. At any rate, if you're having a heart attack, you don't stop to make notes on your music before you keel over."

There was another silence, but he finally broke it.

"A man," he said, "regardless of his faults, virtues, degree of talent, or importance in the general scheme of things, was, a few hours ago, playing Ravel. He will never play Ravel, or anything else, again. Whether the obliteration was achieved through cardiovascular failure, yellow fever, or the sticking of pins in a little rag doll, doesn't modify the outrage."

Greenfield, it must be said, was opposed to death in general. But the death of a *musician* was something for which he found it impossible to forgive whoever or whatever was responsible.

"It modifies," I said, "if he didn't die of natural causes."

"He was playing fast tennis in the hot sun and, according to you, racing Sorrel in the pool."

"But Sorrel is alive and well. And older."

"Conductors have formidable longevity. Toscanini. Stokowski. Fiedler. Monteux. Koussevitzky . . ."

"Come on, Charlie, you know it's a possibility. What with decks collapsing and cars being run off the road."

"I've noticed since the Victoria Hollis business you've had an appetite for the sensational."

He was referring to a case of near-fatal hit-and-run involving a delivery boy of the Sloan's Ford *Reporter,* when he, Greenfield, had sworn personally to track down the criminal who'd left young Peter Kittell lying in a coma on a dark road, and by God, did actually work it out, thanks to his mental agility and my nervous but ceaseless efforts as a spy.

"You're on the alert for crime wherever you go," he went on. "You're addicted."

"Me? I'm not on the alert for anything. I'm on vacation." I knew who was on the alert, all right.

"Hmm," he said.

As we passed Mr. Avery's house, I saw his truculent silhouette against the light spilling through the screen door, the profile turned inquisitively toward the Damaskins' windows. The mangy dog was nowhere in sight.

"Somehow," I said, "I find it hard to believe Mr. Avery is keeping his loud animal locked away out of respect."

"Even Atilla must have had his civilized moments," Greenfield muttered.

When Nadia opened the door to us, she was as self-possessed and gracious as ever, her pointed chin tilted up, her improbable black hair smooth and shining, wearing a tunic and pants of peacock green that gave her a slightly oriental look. But her dark eyes were sombre and a little wary.

"Come in, come in, come in. We will all have a drink and talk about this terrible thing, because if we try to ignore it, it will only be worse."

She accepted the bottle of wine with an appreciative "Perfect!" and led us into the comfortable, eclectic living room where New England furnishings fought with Chinese screens, Israeli wall hangings, African masks, and a huge samovar. Shura was transferring ice cubes from a plastic tray into an ice bucket, his shock having metamorphosed into a bravura anguish.

"From bad to worse!" he announced, "and from worse to rotten! There is something sinister going on, believe me! Macabre! Diabolical! Darkness and evil!"

"Oh, Shura, for God's sake," Nadia said, handing around glasses.

"Am I wrong?" Shura demanded of Greenfield.

Greenfield said, "A man died. It happens frequently."

"Not just died!" Shura came close to him and lowered his voice dramatically. "When a man dies, usually they know from what. You know what happened there, after you left? A doctor comes, examines him, says, 'I have no idea why this man died,' and runs to the phone and calls the police!"

"Not the police," Nadia put in, "the medical examiner."

"He's a *police* doctor, isn't he? That means the *police!*"

Greenfield said, carefully, "He's required to do that by law, whenever there's no clear cause of death."

"No clear cause! Exactly! No clear cause!" Shura came to a full stop, as though he'd made an irrefutable point.

Greenfield leaned back on the country-chintz sofa, took a slow sip of his drink, and said, with an immense calm which indicated to me that his adrenaline was definitely flowing.

"Shura. It only means, that in order to find the cause, they'll have to do a portmortem."

"Ah-hah!" Shura cried, "cut him up! That's what happened! They take him to the hospital, they open him up—and they find nothing! Heart like an ox! Nothing wrong!"

Greenfield sat very still, his eyes on Shura's flushed face.

"Nothing!" Shura repeated. "Found absolutely nothing wrong with the heart!"

I waited to find out what they *had* found. A bullet hole? A stab wound? (A little rag doll full of pinpricks?)

"He was in perfect health!" Shura cried, as though this were the last straw.

"Perfect!" Nadia scoffed. "If it was perfect, would he be dead?"

Greenfield said, "They have methods of determining what happened. Blood tests and so on." He looked annoyed with himself for not having a medical degree.

"How is Mrs. Damaskin?" I asked.

"When they came to tell Fran," Nadia said, "she fainted three times. I stayed with her. The doctor put her to sleep. Then Dorothy Batista stayed with her. Now her sister is there."

"First Batista's deck," Shura moaned, "then Tsuji's car, then the letter, then the ink on the oboe part—" He shook his head. "We are all getting very nervous, Charlie. Morale is very bad. Very bad. Especially in the string section."

Greenfield accepted a tiny hot cheese turnover from the tray Nadia was offering and looked at it thoughtfully.

"If you're suggesting," he said, "that someone is trying to wipe out the entire orchestra, you'd have to convince me there's a reasonable motive."

"Who needs a reasonable motive today? There are terrorists all over the place. Are they reasonable?"

"What sort of terrorists did you have in mind? Rock groups or disco fanatics? Why should they bother, they control the recording industry and the airwaves, classical music will never dethrone them. Disgruntled contemporary composers? If they're upset at not getting enough exposure, it

would hardly serve their cause to diminish the number of
musicians available for the purpose. Or do you think the
KGB has decided systematically to destroy all American cultural organizations that might tempt their artists to defect?
Believe me, if they had, it would be done much more expedi-
tiously. And if you're imagining some perfectionist who feels
the BSO is not doing justice to Brahms or Prokofiev or Ravel,
I can only think of three people who might possibly find a
flaw in your magnificent performance—and Brahms, Prokofiev, and Ravel are all incapacitated."

I was impressed with the amount of thought Greenfield
had obviously given to a possibility he hadn't even considered.

"What did Damaskin say to Holchek, just before he collapsed?"

"Said he was not well, very dizzy. Holchek told him to
leave." Shura sighed.

Greenfield said, "Well, there's no basis yet for assuming
Damaskin didn't simply die from some organic malfunc-
tion."

"At last," said Nadia, "someone is talking sense."

"My God," Shura said, "Noll." He shook his head again.
"You should have seen Fran. Her face was like putty. Poor
Fran. Poor Noll." His head was bent over the old flat-topped
brassbound trunk that served as a coffee table. He slapped it
with his hand. "And now, what do I do with this?"

Greenfield and I looked down at the trunk and then up at
Nadia who was offering cold eggplant spread on small slices
of black bread.

"You just pick it up," she said crisply to Shura, "and walk
over to the house and give it to her."

"How can I give it to her," Shura demanded with a
sweeping gesture toward the Damaskin house, "when she's
lying there full of dope and unconscious and asleep?"

"Then leave it there. It's her property now."

"Leave it? Who will look after it? How will I prove I gave
it back if a thief takes it while she's sleeping?"

I was finding it hard to follow this debate. How could

Shura carry that trunk all the way to the Damaskins' house, and who would want to steal it?

"The sister is there," Nadia said, "and no one is going to accuse us of anything; we are not peasants for God's sake, Shura."

"I have to deliver it into her hands!" Shura insisted. "In front of witnesses! You don't leave a Guarnerius lying around the house like a pair of socks!"

Nadia bristled. "When did you ever see socks lying around my house?"

Greenfield was staring down at the trunk the way Berenson might have stared at a veiled easel in a Florentine studio.

"Damaskin's Guarnerius?" he asked. "In there?"

Shura removed the bowls and plates sitting on the chest, produced a key from his pocket, fitted it to the large brass lock, and threw back the lid. Inside, a violin case reposed on a bed of table linen. He lifted it out, opened it, and took out the violin, gently.

It didn't look like a very impressive instrument to me, but Greenfield reached out and touched it with one reverent finger. Shura showed us the label, with the monogram IHS and above it the sign of the cross.

"Italian Historical Society?" I asked. "Instrument Has Strings? What does it mean?"

"Greek abbreviation," Greenfield said, "for Jesus."

"It means a genuine del Gesù," Nadia said. "That was his mark."

"The dark varnish . . ." Greenfield said with satisfaction.

Shura nodded. "No time for the fancy things. Varnish too dark, one f-hole different from the other, the purfling—" he touched the molding of the outer rim, "not so good. But the *tone!* The *balance!*"

Greenfield took a breath and said, "Play it."

Shura shook his head. "I'm a cellist."

"A few notes," Greenfield insisted.

"It needs Paganini. Not only for his big hands." But he took the bow from the case, swung the violin to his bearded chin like Rhett sweeping Scarlett up those stairs, and played three bars of Mendelssohn.

It was the most mellow resonance I'd ever heard a single instrument produce.

"Like Heifetz playing the *David*," Greenfield murmured.

"Like the *David*, but not like Heifetz." Shura put the violin and bow carefully back in the case, looking down covetously at the too-dark, imperfectly purfled instrument.

So much for poor Noll, I thought. By acquiring the Guarnerius he arranged that his death should play second fiddle to his violin. I was about to ask a pertinent question, but Greenfield got there first.

"What is Damaskin's Guarnerius doing in your trunk?"

"He was nervous about it," Shura said, "with all these strange things going on. Everyone knew he had it, he was afraid something would happen. He had no place to lock it up. He asked me as a favor—" He stopped and sighed.

"Noel and his favors," Nadia said sadly.

"Well, now he's dead," Shura said. "No more favors. He's dead, and I don't even know if he told Fran he gave me the Guarnerius to keep here. She could already think it was stolen. What a situation! What a situation!"

"You are making a mountain out of nothing," Nadia said. "Such nonsense. Come, let's go to the table, my dinner will be spoiled."

She fed us a delicious cold sour soup with paper-thin slices of cucumber floating in it, which I'd always known as "schav."

"You know what these green leaves are," Nadia said, "they are *sorrel*. Like our guest conductor. People either love it or they hate it. Like our guest conductor. Some people call it sourweed. The sourness is supposed to stimulate the appetite."

Like our Eleanor, I thought.

The soup was followed by thinly sliced veal in a delicately flavored sauce, a salad, and finally strawberries the size of small apples, floating in sweet cream and nutmeg. The sorrel must have done its work, because in spite of the distressing situation, we all managed to eat a reasonable amount. And Nadia determinedly kept the conversation to impersonal musical speculation: Could Mehta bring back the sheen of glamor to the New York Philharmonic? What were the odds on Beverly Sills' making a go of the New York City Opera? Who could have spread the rumor that Rampal had picked a fight with Galway? Would anyone be playing Copland a hundred years from now?

But inevitably we got back to the Damaskins.

"Almost ten o'clock," Shura said, "I wonder if they heard anything yet. From the hospital."

"I think we should see if Fran woke up," Nadia decided. "Maybe she would eat something. Shura, go and see."

Shura hesitated, torn between his natural compassion and his need for reassurance on one side, and his fear of learning something far from reassuring on the other. Finally, reluctantly, he put down his coffee cup and went toward the kitchen. We heard the back screen door slam.

"She went to the camp just this morning to see the son," Nadia said, "which is not far from here, some very exclusive place. The son is—how old is he?—fourteen, fifteen. He is a skinny boy, with not a nice disposition. They will have trouble with him. Well, *Fran* will have trouble. Their only child. Very spoiled. But so was Noel. Noel was like a spoiled child. Give me your cup, Maggie." She poured more coffee. "Yes, for Noel everything must always be the best. In Boston they must live in Chestnut Hill . . . oriental rugs and a marble fireplace. To eat, he must go to the most *chic* restaurants, on tour he must always have the *best* room, at parties he would speak only to the *important* people—*important* was very important to Noel. He was not going to remain only in the first violins, he was going to be much more important. A conductor. A star. That was his plan." She sighed. "He had the idea he was special. Where he got this idea I don't know, he was not special. Very good, but not special. But he expected always to get everything he wanted—there are people like that. And he would get it, just because he expected. Like that party last night. Madelyn told me she did not invite them. But Noel thinks 'Who would not want me?' He invites himself. Then he leaves in the middle for this coaching business—no problem, we will take care of Fran—I've seen this type many times, they drop their clothes on the floor and somebody else must always pick them up. And Fran did not help the situation, nothing but the best for her Noel, she was infatuated, like a schoolgirl, hanging on his arm—oh well . . ."

The screen door slammed and Shura burst into the room. In the short distance between the two houses he had somehow managed to acquire the ragged, spent look of a man who had crossed a continent on horseback. He pointed a trembling hand toward the house he'd just left.

"You know who is there? Police! The chief of police! And the police doctor—"

"Medical examiner," Nadia corrected automatically.

"And some men from the District Attorney!" He collapsed into a chair. "My God. They must have found something. I told you. I told you there was something terrible happening here!"

As we left the Charnovs' house some thirty minutes later, Greenfield directed a thoughtful scowl at the Damaskins' driveway, the police car and the pale green Buick standing there, took his wallet from his pants pocket, withdrew a card, glanced at it, and said, "Do you have a pen?"

I opened the door of the Honda and slipped off the ball-point attached to the visor. "What's going on, Charlie?" I asked, knowing full well.

He looked at the ballpoint. "Like writing with a carrot," he grumbled, and crossed the grass to the Damaskins' driveway, peered down at the trunk of the Buick, and scribbled. I got into the Honda and rolled the windows down all the way. It was a lot warmer tonight than it had been the night before. I heard scuffling sounds behind me and turned to look: a large furry dog of an indeterminate breed was pulling a woman up the road on the end of a leash.

Greenfield came back across the grass and maneuvered himself into the passenger seat with a grunt that condemned my inexcusable lack of foresight in owning a vehicle so deficient in leg room. I started up, released the hand brake, and shifted into reverse, then slammed my foot on the other brake. The large furry dog was heading straight for the back of the Honda, the woman holding for dear life onto the leash and shouting "No! No! Daisy! No!"

But Daisy kept going, around the back of the car and straight up to my window where she stood up on her hind legs and planted her front paws on the frame, her tail going like a metronome, her tongue hanging out like a wet flag, and a grin of victory on her bedraggled face.

"Down, Daisy! Down, down!" It was the hollow-chested young mother with the eager smile who had not been able to give us directions the night before. "I'm terribly sorry! She's never *done* this before! Oh—hello. I see you found that house you were looking for."

"Yes. Thank you. Um—nice dog."

"Oh yes, she's a darling. Sit down, Daisy. Sit. Sit. Yes, she's just wonderful with the children. I don't know what possessed her to come into this driveway, she gave me quite a scare doing that just as you started your car, especially after what happened to that other dog. Not that *he's* a loss. I shouldn't say it, but I can't help feeling relieved that he— Sit, Daisy! That's a good girl. Yes, it was awful. I mean even though it was a nasty dog, you don't like to see an animal run over—"

Greenfield, who had been silent upon his peak in Darien, turned his head to look at her.

I said, "You don't mean the dog that belongs to—uh—to the house just over there?"

"Mr. Avery. Yes."

You didn't have to be in the neighborhood long, I gathered, to know Mr. Avery.

"Like master, like dog, they say, not much to choose between them. Still, it's a shame, a living creature, you know. Sit, Daisy!"

"What happened?"

"Well, the dog was barking away this morning, as usual,

and then the man in this next house—well, according to my little boy, that man was taking his car out of the garage and the dog ran into his driveway, barking away, and the man just backed the car right over the dog. I'm really sorry my little boy saw it, because, you know, those things stay with a child. Even though he didn't like the dog. Daisy, sit! I see the police are there. Mr. Avery must be making quite a fuss about it. No, Daisy, no! Sit. Sit. Oh dear, she wants her walk, I guess."

I guess she did, because the young mother was catapulted into the night by sixty-five pounds of happy fur.

I met Greenfield's eye—slightly glazed and full of conjecture. We sat in silence for a few moments.

"So," I said finally, "Mr. Avery has this magic cloak, which renders him invisible. He puts it on, goes to Tanglewood, walks out onstage in the midst of rehearsal, gives Damaskin the evil eye, which he also happens to possess, thereby killing Damaskin and avenging the death of his dog, not to mention those tortured hours listening to Damaskin's music."

He said, "I'd like to stop at the police station in Lenox."

"Right. I think they should know about that cloak."

I pulled out of the driveway and drove to Lenox. No point in asking Greenfield what he was up to; he had pulled up his mental drawbridge and there was no way over the moat.

We found the police station, after inquiring as to its whereabouts from a gas station attendant who had plenty of time on his hands since he had stopped pumping gas at seven P.M. and was merely using the office phone to call his girlfriend. Police Headquarters consisted of a side door in the immaculate red-brick, white-trim Town Hall next to the Fire Department. The door was locked and there was a sign on it saying the officer in charge would be back shortly, please leave any messages at the Fire House next door. Lenox, Mass., was obviously a high-crime district.

Greenfield went over to the Fire House to determine how long it would be before the police force returned, and he had barely made the round trip when the officer in charge appeared, holding a container of hot coffee. Greenfield told him he needed some information, and the officer, looking at us suspiciously, opened the door, let us enter ahead of him, told us to wait, unlocked another door and went through it, and appeared on the other side of a window cut into the partition separating us from him. He sat down at the desk behind the window and said, "What kind of information?"

"Earlier this evening," Greenfield said, "I parked on one of the side streets and when I returned to the car I was hemmed in, front and back. In maneuvering my way out I'm afraid I scraped the fender of the car in front of me. It wasn't a bad scrape, but I would like to apologize to the owner and offer to pay the repair cost. I left my name and number under the wiper, but I haven't heard from anyone— it's possible the slip of paper was removed, or blown away, before the owner could see it. At any rate, I had written down the license number and I was hoping there would be some way of tracing it." He handed the officer the small white card on which he had scribbled with my ballpoint.

The officer, who had listened to this recital as though he were a soldier in the front lines being confronted by Mary Poppins, took the card and said, brusquely, "Tracing a license number takes a lot of—" Then he looked at the number and said, "Oh. That's the doc's car. Yeah. Well. Could I have your name, please, and where you're staying."

He didn't even *ask* if Greenfield was a resident. We obviously melted into the local population like Americans in Moscow.

The officer wrote a name and address on a separate piece of paper and handed it and the card to Greenfield, who thanked him, and we left.

"I don't know why you're not at the Berkshire Playhouse," I said. "They could use you in *Our Town*."

Greenfield got into the car and said, "If you continue down Main Street I'll show you how to get to Stockbridge without taking the longer route."

"I'm not going to Stockbridge," I said firmly, "I'm going back to my room to pack."

"Pack what?"

"My clothes into my suitcase. I don't like packing first thing in the morning, I forget things."

He looked at me for a long moment, then settled casually back in the seat and said, in the quiet voice that means you might as well stop struggling because he's going to prevail in the end, "This won't take long. Just continue down Main Street."

I started the car. "At least when those galley slaves were pulling on the oars, they knew where they were going and why."

"I doubt it. In any case, since you're leaving tomorrow, it doesn't concern you."

"Oh, that's *really* low."

"Watch the road, please."

We pulled up, eventually, in front of a well-kept lawn in Stockbridge, stretching from the street far back to a comfortable-looking white house with green shutters. There was one light in an upstairs room; otherwise the house was dark, and there was no sign of a pale green Buick.

"He's not back," I said, "and for all we know he'll be out all night. How long do you intend to skulk here in the dark?"

"Give it five minutes." He got out of the car and wandered slowly up and down the sidewalk. I looked at my watch. At one point he stopped next to my window, said conversationally, "I understand it's ninety-three degrees in Sloan's Ford. And humid," and resumed his wandering.

So that was his game. Well, he could think again. I was on vacation.

"The five minutes are up," I said, and turned the key in the ignition, whereupon the pale green Buick passed me on the right and cut across into a driveway leading to the house.

And Greenfield, by God, watched it as though he had actually deduced the time of arrival, when it was nothing but sheer dumb luck.

I got out of the car as Greenfield went up the drive to

speak to the man who was climbing out of the Buick, and stood uncertainly on the sidewalk watching them exchange words. Then Greenfield turned and said, "Maggie—" and I started up the drive only to hear him add, "I'll be out in a few minutes."

In the moment before they turned to go inside, I saw "the doc" looking at me. He was a stocky man, sixtyish, no glamor to speak of, with a face that was not surprised by much and wasn't going to be too solemn about anything it encountered; the mouth hovered on the brink of irony, the clever eyes glinted with humor, the body was relaxed and capable, and the casual look he gave me was wicked. Eleanor would never in a million years have understood it, but he had what was missing in Sorrel.

Then they went inside and there I was standing alone in the light from the upstairs window. I felt like one of those anonymous chauffeurs who lean against their limousines for hours while the elite do whatever it is they've taken a fancy to do. I went back to the car, stewing. I had a good mind to take off and leave him there. Let him try whistling up a taxi at eleven P.M. on this quiet small-town road.

I looked back at the house. There was now a light in the front downstairs window. I decided to trade resentment for resourcefulness, and went quietly back across the lawn and sidled up to the window. All I could see through a slit in the venetian blind was a piece of the doctor's framed certificate on the wall. But I could hear fairly well, and what I heard was the doctor's voice.

". . . pathologist found nothing. Heart valves normal, heart muscle normal, coronary arteries, aorta and pulmonary, all normal . . . no abnormalities . . . toxicologic exam . . . good man in the lab here . . . chemist . . . specializes in abnormal findings, he's a nut about little-known toxic substances, so on . . . sends me this pathology report, 'looks like' and 'could be'—you know . . . well, not enough to make a firm diagnosis, but if there's a suspicion of homicide, hell, we move it right along. . . . Got the specimen over to the state police night crew . . . they should have it in the Boston lab by morning. . . . Should have a confirmation—or otherwise—within forty-eight hours."

Greenfield's voice: "In the meantime—?"

Doctor's voice: "Doctor, I can *smell* homicide."

I crept back to the car. "*Doctor?*" Doctor *who?* Then the really relevant word hit me. Homicide.

I got into the car. Of course, that's what it had been leading up to all the time, but still, one never fully believed in the reality of such things while there was still a chance of alternative explanations.

The front door opened and Greenfield came out and down to the car. It would not have been obvious to the uninitiated, but to me there was definitely a qualitative change in the slouch and the disconsolate expression, which hadn't been there since he'd locked up the office. Lacking only the mad exaltation, the lance, the spavined horse, and the little fat man on the donkey, this was the Spanish don reborn.

He still, however, spoke English.

"Let's go," he said, fitting himself into the seat.

"Where to," I asked, starting the car, "the hospital? You have surgery scheduled at this late hour? Doctor?" I looked up and down the empty street and made a U-turn.

There was an ominous silence from Greenfield and then, "It would be fatuous to object to eavesdropping per se. Under the circumstances I can't even object to it on moral or ethical grounds. But when it isn't absolutely necessary, it's just a little inelegant."

"Not to mention uncomfortable. But then, I wasn't invited in. By the way, I tuned in too late to hear what alias you were using. You'd better tell me, I wouldn't want to spoil the fun out here in Dashiell Hammett country."

"Don't be frivolous. The man obviously wasn't going to hand out information to any passing stranger. I had to have an entree, and when dealing with professionals, the best possible course is to refer them to a colleague. I mentioned I was a friend of Winter's. It so happens they attended Cornell simultaneously."

"Ah-ha!" Ralph W. Winter was a resident of Sloan's Ford and a rather well-known cardiologist.

"I also explained I was a friend of Shura's and an acquaintance of Damaskin's. As for his calling me 'Doctor,' that, I suppose, was what he considered humor. I asked a few knowledgeable questions, thanks to the evenings I've spent listening to Winter discourse on his subject."

"I apologize. Well? What did you find out? What did they discover in that lab with that chemist who's such a hotshot with abnormal findings? Why did they send the specimen to Boston? What do they think killed Damaskin?"

There was another pause, and then Greenfield said, "Poison."

I stared at him. "*Really?*" I whispered.

"Keep your eyes on the road."

"*Poison.*" It was such a theatrical word. So unreal.

"It has to be confirmed, but it looks that way."

"What—arsenic? Strychnine?"

"Evidently something more esoteric."

"Incredible."

We rolled through the night for a while in silence.

"I gather nobody's considering suicide as a possibility."

"If they are, it's a fruitless speculation. You met the man. He wouldn't have taken a hair from his own head, much less his life."

"Well," I said, vindicated, "I told you it didn't look like a heart attack."

"In a sense it was. His heart was ultimately attacked."

"You always tell me not to quibble."

"There's a difference between quibbling and being precise."

"Of course. *Precise* refers to employer and *quibble* to employee." He sighed. I turned into Wheatleigh Drive, waiting for Greenfield to begin the circuitous verbal journey to the destination I was fairly certain he had in mind.

"What time," he asked, finally, "does Elliot usually go to bed?"

My God! *Elliot?*

"Charlie. What are you getting at?"

"It's a simple question. If the medical examiner, who doesn't even know me, can give me his professional findings, surely you can answer one innocuous question."

"Why do you want to know?"

"Maggie. It's eleven fifteen. Would he be asleep or not?"

"It depends. Why?"

"Would you say he's quite a self-sufficient man, your husband? Able to look after himself in a pinch? When he's traveling, for instance, with no one taking his shirts to the laundry, arranging his meals and so on, he manages to survive?"

I was obviously not going to achieve the short-cut. I would either have to follow him through his maze, his geometric pattern of verbal paths among the hedges, each one leading into yet another, then doubling back, going around in circles—or squares—and seemingly getting nowhere, or I'd have to come right out and answer the unspoken question, and I wasn't going to chance that I was wrong.

"Charlie," I said, pulling into the parking space opposite the tower, "please, just for once, take the shortest route between what you want me to do and how you're going to tell me."

He got out of the car. I followed. He stood looking at the tower, and I assumed that was just another way of stalling, until I noticed he wasn't *looking*, he was *peering*, and I followed his gaze. The tower stood there, a wraithlike silver column among the trees, with little black gaps where the tiny windows were, and a larger gap where the door led out to the balcony eighty-five feet up. I saw nothing to peer at.

"What do you see?" I asked.

"Nothing. A flicker of the imagination." He walked up the steps to the garden. I hurried after him and around him and stood in his path.

"Come on, Charlie, out with it!"

He scowled. "You're old enough to know that aggression is not the most effective weapon in the female arsenal."

"Too bad. It's late and I have to pack."

"You don't *have* to pack. You *choose* to pack." He circled me and continued up the path to the front portico.

"People usually take their belongings with them," I said, catching up, "when they leave to go home."

"What if you were obliged to stay a few more days?"

At last! We were coming out of the maze.

"There's no obligation involved," I said. "I'm on vacation."

He stopped halfway along the portico and turned on me, slowly, quietly, a highly civilized man who also happened to be a volcano.

"If even the Knights of Columbus," he said, "or the Associated Tool and Die Workers' Bowling League was being threatened, and I were in a position to do something about it, I'd feel obligated. If even the lives of all the television decision-makers in southern California were under attack and I might be able to help, I'd feel obligated. When the aggregation in jeopardy is the instrument that creates one of the few illuminations in a predominantly murky world, obligation is a meagre word."

Humility was not one of Greenfield's salient characteristics; he never questioned his ability to tackle problems of inordinate size and complexity. It was the *small* details of living that got him down. Instruct the UN? *Any* day. Hang a curtain? Forget it.

On the other hand, his moral sense was unerring. Mine was, of necessity, flexible. He was perfectly right that if, indeed, the BSO was threatened, and if, indeed, we had the necessary equipment to help, conscience demanded action. But were they, and did we? Easy enough for him to define imperatives, he was stuck here anyway. I had family responsibilities; I had a flower bed half finished; I had an invitation, with Elliot, to spend Sunday on a friend's sailboat.

"Charlie," I said, "just because we got lucky with Victoria Hollis doesn't give us a graduate degree in crime detection."

"Crime detection," he said with irritable deliberation, "is largely a matter of combining physical activity with the intelligent and informed application of life experience, to tackle a problem with which any acute mind, trained in the art of thinking, can eventually cope. Since you are reasonably active, we have the necessary resources."

"So gallant."

The door of the separate apartment at the end of the portico opened and a head poked out. Madame Sorrel, icy but polite.

"Please, if you don't mind—"

"Oh!" I said, "I'm sorry! I hope we didn't disturb Mr. Sorrel. Please give him our apologies."

Her lips twitched in an odd little smile. "It wasn't he who heard you." She closed the door quietly.

We left the portico and went past the fountain to the front doors and into the Hall. There was no one around, but I heard voices and music in the bar.

I said, "Listen, I'm sure the local police are perfectly capable, not to mention the District Attorney's men—"

"I'm sure they are," he said, taking a deep breath, "but this isn't the only crime they have to deal with, and time is important. There's more than one way to destroy an orchestra. Disintegrating morale is contagious and pernicious."

"You really think it's a plot?"

"I haven't begun to *think*. I'm *preparing* to think."

Then he brought out the big gun. "If these incidents *are* connected, there are one hundred and five targets on that Tanglewood stage. And one of them is a friend."

Shura! That hadn't occurred to me. Was Shura a target? Immediately, the impossible became possible, the impersonal problem personal.

"But what can we do? Where would we start? There are thousands of people roaming around Tanglewood—how could we even *begin* to trace—?" I dropped onto the sofa, limp with anticipated fatigue.

"You'd better tell them in the office," Greenfield said, "that you'll be keeping the room. And you'd better call Elliot—if he's still awake." He took his room key from his pocket and added, dryly, "Working in your kitchen is, in any case, no way to spend a vacation."

"Kitchen and work," I said, "are compatible. Tanglewood and work are not. Staying here and working is like going to the Four Seasons when you're on the Scarsdale Diet."

I thought I had him that time, but as he moved toward the corridor to his room, he murmured, "I don't know where you get those trashy similes."

I went to the office. I went to the telephone in the corridor. I called home.

"Elliot," I said, "listen—"

7

It was still very warm the next morning, even at seven o'clock. I opened my eyes to see that at some point in my restless sleep I'd kicked off the single sheet with which I'd been covered. I lay there for a few minutes, gazing out the casement window at the upper branches of trees on which the sunlit leaves were not even faintly stirring. The two halves of my bikini still sat on the windowsill where I'd spread them to dry. I decided that since I was now at the mercy of any schedule Greenfield might impose, I'd better get my swimming in before breakfast.

There was no one at the pool at that quiet, private hour of the morning. Except for one yellow butterfly darting among the wildflowers that grew between the rocks on the slope, I had the little green dell to myself, and I slipped into the pool, gasping as I hit the cold water. After an energetic twenty minutes I was thoroughly awake and hungry, and dripped my way back up the garden.

I saw Greenfield sprawled in the big rustic chair on his balcony, wearing a bright green knit shirt and his chino pants, pen in hand, frowning down at a yellow pad on his lap, mentally pursuing a killer. It was a wrench, after playing down below with the butterflies, to face the unpleasant reality of what had happened, and it took me a while to make the transition.

I sidetracked to the balcony and said, "The architecture's okay, but you're a little mature for the part, and anyway, the way it goes, you're supposed to be down here and the girl up there."

He looked down at me with the same interest he might have shown a passing squirrel.

"When you saw Sorrel and Damaskin on the tennis court," he said, "what was going on?"

Was he serious?

"They were playing golf," I said.

He looked at me with the air of a man climbing Everest who has just been handed the *Sunday Times* to deliver on the way.

"If I were in the market for humor," he said, "I'd read some campaign oratory. *How* were they playing? How many were on the court? Was anyone else in the vicinity? Did they stop playing at any time while you were there?"

"They were playing singles. Mrs. Sorrel was watching. Nobody else was there. They stopped once, to change sides."

"Was Mrs. Sorrel doing anything other than watching?"

"You mean knitting or something? No. She was just sitting there." I dabbed at my wet hair with the towel.

"Was there anything on the bench or the ground that resembled a thermos, a flask, a cup, or anything that might have contained food?"

"Oh my God. No, there wasn't." Poison, I thought. Poison in the food, poison in the drink—I looked up at the sunlight sparkling on the trees against a summer-blue sky and found the incongruity appalling. "Charlie," I said, "I'm dripping and I haven't had breakfast. I'll be with you in half an hour."

He seemed to notice for the first time that I was neither dry nor clad.

"In the meantime," he said, tearing a sheet from the yellow pad and handing it to me, "write down whatever you can remember of yesterday's conversation at the pool."

What meantime? I ate breakfast by tackling my grapefruit, poached eggs, and coffee with my left hand and recording as much as I could recall of the Sorrel–Damaskin exchanges with my right, finding it difficult to concentrate, because it was evident, in the dining room, that the dramatic events of the last rehearsal had made the rounds. Heads leaned close to other heads, speculation and reminiscence flew in muted tones from mouth to ear. The tennis quartet gobbled its wheat cakes and corn muffins, thrilled from sweatband to sneaker by this unanticipated vacation bonus. (In October they would be saying to their dinner guests, "We were *there* when it *happened*. Just a few hours before, he was *swimming* not ten feet away from me!) The elderly trio was deeply shocked, the one in the bed jacket indicating, in a tone of severe disapproval, that dying at rehearsal was simply not done in her day. The Felkers were arguing in stage whispers over their prunes and cereal, Mrs. Felker apparently assuming that this episode had occurred for the express purpose of serving as a warning to Felker to take more time off from work and not to smoke cigars. It seemed that as far as anyone at Wheatleigh knew, Damaskin had died of a heart attack.

Only a few minutes beyond the half-hour I was back with Greenfield, sitting on his balcony, watching him scan the yellow sheet I'd given back to him. There were yellow sheets all over the balcony, some on the wooden table, some on his lap, some crumpled up and discarded on the floor. There was also a blue booklet, issued by the Council of the BSO, titled "Know Your Orchestra." I picked it up and glanced through it. It contained pictures and short biographies of all the orchestra musicians.

Greenfield dropped my yellow sheet on the table, leaned back in his chair, gazed out at the garden, and began, slowly and repeatedly, to tap the blunt end of his pen against the arm of his chair, a practice that seems to aid him in thinking —or preparing to think, as the case may be.

Finally he said, "The question of whether Damaskin's death is linked to the other incidents, and therefore indicates some lunatic plot against the BSO, can only be answered by discovering how and why Damaskin was killed, and by whom."

"We know *how*," I said.

"In that case you know more than I do. I only know what the agent was, not how and when it was administered."

"Well, if it was poison, he either had to eat it or drink it."

"Unless," Greenfield agreed dryly, "there's a Bulgarian around with a specially constructed umbrella. And I don't see Damaskin as having been a threat to any foreign government. He would never knowingly have put himself at risk." He shuffled the papers on the table and finally extracted one. "Timetable for yesterday," he said. "The doctor gave five or six hours as the outside limit for the poison to take effect. That eliminates anything that took place before eleven A.M. yesterday. Between eleven and five Damaskin did the following: Midway through morning rehearsal he took a coffee break. Immediately after rehearsal he drove home with Shura, arriving there approximately ten of one; he disappeared into his house for as long as it took him to change into tennis clothes, not more than five minutes, at which point he reappeared, drove Shura's car to Wheatleigh, arriving at one twenty, and repaired to the tennis court to meet Sorrel—"

"How do you know that?"

"I know that," he said, with the look of one who is no stranger to ill-treatment, "because of your obsession with walking, which left me at the mercy of other people's arrangements. In order to get a lift back to Wheatleigh, I was forced to ride all the way to the Charnovs' and back again, because Shura had promised to lend Damaskin the car so that he could keep his tennis date with Sorrel."

"If you were in better shape you could have walked back and saved a lot of time."

"The shape I'm in," he said, "is perfectly adequate for any undertakings I have in mind. Shall I go on, or would you like to check my blood pressure?" I raised my eyes to heaven and he went on. "What time did he get down to the pool?"

"I wasn't looking at my watch, but I'd say about two thirty or two forty. And he left about an hour later, because

I followed him almost immediately, and when I met you outside your room, you said it was a quarter to four. At that point he was—" I stopped, suddenly confronted by the possible import of what I was about to say.

"He was what?"

"He was . . . um . . . coming down the back staircase from the second floor."

Greenfield stared at me for quite a while without seeing me at all. Then he said, "What was he wearing?"

I squinted at the balcony railing, trying to recreate the scene. "Terrycloth tennis shirt over swim trunks, tennis sneakers, and he was carrying his tennis racquet case—he had it with him at the pool."

"So he wasn't invited into the Sorrels' rooms to change," Greenfield said to some invisible person perched in a tree, "either before or after his swim."

"I don't know about before."

"Maggie. Try thinking for a change. Would you take a racquet to the pool if you had somewhere to leave it?"

"Maybe he had something else in the bag that he wanted with him," I said, saving face.

"Did you see him take anything from it?"

"I wasn't watching his every move. Nobody warned me he was going to end the day in the postmortem room."

In just such a careless way we do make our most significant observations, inevitably failing to recognize them, and thereby wasting a lot of time.

Greenfield drew a doodle on a yellow sheet and said, "He came down from the second floor . . . *whatever* . . . he was doing there . . . at almost four. We have to assume he went home at that point, since he arrived at rehearsal fully clothed. He must have arrived at rehearsal at least five minutes before it started, and it takes twenty minutes to get from here to his house, leaving him not much more than five minutes to change—in fact, he was running around, back and forth, upstairs and downstairs, around the court and in and out of the pool, covering a great deal of territory in a relatively short space of time on a hot, sunny day—" He threw down the pen in disgust. "The man died of a heart attack. It wouldn't be the first medical error in history."

"You're not serious."

"No." He sighed and picked up another yellow sheet. "Between eleven o'clock yesterday morning and five o'clock yesterday afternoon, Damaskin visited three possible sources of food and drink. They all have to be checked out. The number of people—as far as we know—who had more than a casual acquaintance with him, and who were present at one or more of those food-and-drink sources—" His shoulders sagged a little more than usual, "That number, conservatively, is one hundred and eight."

I felt a headache coming on.

"Well, that's not so bad," I said. "If we work fast, say one a day, we could eliminate most of them in three months."

He ignored me. "I've reduced it to four. In the interests of sanity." He handed me the yellow sheet. "Do your best." He got up and went into his room.

I looked at the list of instructions and the four names, written in Greenfield's very best illegible hand. One of the names surprised me because it was ridiculous and another because I would never have thought to include it.

"Charlie," I said, going after him, "you don't mean it. You want me to check on *Fran Damaskin?* Why not Santa Claus while you're at it? That woman was *infatuated* with her husband. Even Nadia said so."

"Only one thing about the human animal is certain. Ever."

"And this man in the orchestra? Just because he had words with Noel? If every man who can't take a joke killed the person who made it, there'd be no such thing as overpopulation."

"You have a good deal to learn," he said, fishing for something in a drawer of the chest, "about the intensity of feeling that circulates among musicians in an orchestra. Try imagining nineteen actors adrift in a lifeboat with a producer." He shut the drawer and opened another.

"I don't believe it. *Nothing* is like nineteen actors. Also, I don't understand this reference to gardening."

With consummate patience Greenfield went out to the balcony, returned with the blue booklet, opened it, found the page he wanted, handed it to me, and went back to his drawer.

I read the short biographical note next to the picture of the man with the thick eyeglasses and the jowls.

"Joseph Holchek joined the BSO in 1949. . . . Born in Prague, March of 1916 . . . an early interest in chemistry gave way to his love for music . . . studied with Moldow in Vienna. . . . He is an avid horticulturist and bird watcher. . . ."

"Wow," I said, "flowers and birds. Sounds like a real homicidal maniac."

"The operative word," he said, shutting the second drawer, "is chemistry. Do you have any Cutter's?"

"What kind of cutters? You mean scissors?"

"I'm acquainted with the word *scissors*. If I meant scissors—" He ran a hand through his gray hair, leaving it standing on end. "Cutter's. Insect repellent. I've left mine at home."

"No. You said we weren't going to the African interior, so I didn't bother."

"I'd appreciate it if you'd pick up a bottle while you're making the rounds. Not just insect repellent. Cutter's."

"They're all more or less the sa—"

"Cutter's."

He was like that. He attached himself to products and nothing would separate him from them but termination of their manufacture. Palmolive was the only soap. Parker 51 fountain pen was the only writing instrument. When Betty Crocker's Date Bar Mix unaccountably disappeared forever from the shelves he was inconsolable for a year. Helen Deutch, whom he had conscripted to bake them weekly after she'd once thoughtlessly brought them to the office, tried thirty-seven substitutes to no avail.

He had plopped his suitcase on the bed and was probing

the interior to make certain no overlooked plastic bottle lurked in its corners.

"It's eight thirty," he said. "Take care of those first three items and I'll meet you at the car in an hour."

I left the room and went down the corridor to the Hall.

One of the chambermaids was running a floor polisher over the oak herringbone. Through the front doors I saw the beard, in his short-sleeved white shirt and black pants, taking two expensive cases from the trunk of a silver Porsche while a short middle-aged man in a tight LaCoste T-shirt and faded denims looked up at the Tiffany windows with a satisfied air and a middle-aged woman of mandatory slenderness, with loose brown hair bouncing on her shoulders, a trendy top torn from Gloria Vanderbilt's hands as she was designing it, and no bra, pranced around the fountain with little-girl enthusiasm, saying "I love it, I love it!"

New guests. Got up at the crack of dawn, so they wouldn't waste one precious minute. Or better still, came straight up from Studio 54. I checked the bulletin board and what I was looking for was gone. I could see the beard would be occupied for a while, so I proceeded down the far corridor to the office, and asked the handsome proprietor (also, but more elegantly, bearded) for what I wanted. The dreamily beautiful proprietress looked at me curiously and wandered out on some errand.

"The *what?*" he said. "God knows where it is. In the garbage, probably. Here—" He nudged a wastebasket in my direction. "You can look through that, if you want." The telephone rang and he told some unfortunate soul that all weekends were booked solid until September.

I sorted through the scraps of paper in the basket, and there it was, crumpled up at the bottom. I straightened it out, put it in my pocket, thanked him, and went across the corridor to the dining room, as the beard entered the office to announce the new guests.

The waitresses were all busy, and it was a good while before I managed to snare one.

"I wasn't on for lunch yesterday," she said, and stopped

one of the other girls on her way to the pantry. "Who was on for lunch yesterday? I think Pat was—right, Pat and Trudy. Trudy's off today—you want to talk to Pat?"

Pat came in from the kitchen bearing French toast and I waited until she served it and then took her aside, gave her a fairly accurate verbal picture of Damaskin, and asked if she'd seen anyone of that description at lunch yesterday. She said no, only the elderly trio, and a couple who had once been the proprietors of a rival hostelry, and two non-resident school teachers. I asked who took care of the bar at lunchtime and she said Irene, but she wouldn't be in until later.

I went back to the Hall to wait for the beard, and presently he came jauntily down the grand staircase and grinned at me.

"Hi!" he said. "How was the pool this morning?"

God, the boy had eyes all 'round his head; I hadn't seen *him* earlier that morning. Still, that was all to the good, considering my mission. I asked my questions.

Yes, he knew Mr. Damaskin, he often dropped in for a swim in the pool. The proprietor didn't much care for it, but he didn't say anything, sometimes he even played tennis with Mr. Damaskin. Yes, he'd seen Damaskin yesterday, coming up from the court with the Sorrels. He'd gone into the bar for a few minutes, then used one of the ground-floor public washrooms to change for the pool, and then met the Sorrels in the front portico. No, he hadn't gone into the Sorrels' rooms. Yes, he'd seen him come back from the pool and go up the back staircase—if it had been anyone else, the beard would have stopped him, but Mr. Damaskin wasn't a total stranger, so he figured it was all right. He'd seen him go upstairs once before. When? Last summer. Why did I want to know? What was all this about? He knew Mr. Damaskin was dead—

"I'm doing some medical research," I said, "on heart failure. For an article for the *Reader's Digest.*"

The beard was first impressed, then skeptical. I made a quick getaway.

On the way to Tanglewood (driving this time, the humidity being enough to discourage the most dedicated walker), I gave Greenfield the results of my inquiries and the piece of paper I'd found in the bottom of the office wastebasket. It was the tennis roster from the day before and it hadn't told me a thing. Neither did the "Mm" from Greenfield when he looked at it.

"Mm what?" I asked.

"That tennis date could have been made in any one of three ways. It might have been a last-minute impulse, or it might have been prearranged by Sorrel, or it might have been prearranged by Damaskin. I was interested in knowing which. Now that I've seen it I can only eliminate one possibility. Damaskin didn't arrange it. If he had, he'd certainly have had his name on there."

"You can also eliminate the last-minute impulse. Since Sorrel's name is there he booked the court in advance."

"He could have planned to play with his wife. Substituting Damaskin could have been an impulse."

"Why are we discussing Sorrel anyway? He's a highly respected, well-known conductor, and he obviously didn't know Damaskin all that well—why would he even give him a second thought, let alone—?" I chose not to speak the unspeakable.

"Read your record of their conversation," Greenfield said.

We had reached the Lion's Gate and I pulled onto the grass verge, then walked with Greenfield onto the grounds, trying to reconstruct the conversation in my mind, but I was immediately distracted by the sight of Jenny Springer pointing her camera at a five-foot-eight cello apparently making its way unaided across the lawn, wearing a pair of sneakers. The sneakers proved to belong to a four-foot-nine girl behind it who was transporting the instrument.

"You think she really plays that thing," Jenny asked us as we came up to her, "or they just have her walking around for the tourists to take pictures?" And then, with a surprised smile, "You didn't leave!"

"Change of plans," I said.

Greenfield said he had an appointment and walked off, leaving me with the problem of detaching myself from Jenny so that I could do what had to be done. I asked the standard question.

"Where's your mother?"

"Giving a performance of *Camille* in our room. It's a shame, because it's all being wasted on Nefertiti and she's not a theater-going cat. Wasn't that weird about that violinist dying onstage? I had nightmares about it. In between waking up because my mother was being sick all over the bathroom."

"What's the matter with her?"

Jenny shrugged. "Pale and wan and wasting away. I wanted to get a doctor, but she said no, leave me alone, I'm not sick, it's just nerves. What do you think I should do?"

"Does she have any Valium?"

"Of course. She carries around half a drugstore wherever she goes. But she already took Valium."

"I don't know, Jenny, why don't you wait and see how she is this afternoon?" I looked at my watch. I had people to see and things to sort out in my mind, and I could do without extraneous complications. But Jenny was born to be the bearer of complications. Not satisfied with having transmitted the news of Eleanor's attack of nerves, she grabbed my arm, as we walked up the path toward the Main House, and directed my attention to a group of students on the porch.

"You see that girl, with the long hair?"

It was the Botticelli from the cafeteria. I remembered someone had called her Allison.

"When I first got here," Jenny said, "about a half-hour ago, I was sitting up there on the porch looking over at the Bowl and wondering if I needed a filter, because the sky's pretty bright, and that girl came rushing up—there was nobody else around then—and she tore something off the big bulletin board on the wall and the tears—the tears were running all over her face and she was really crying, out loud, and hitting her hand against the wall, 'No, No, No!' and then she"—Jenny hesitated fractionally—"she tore open the front of her shirt!"

I found myself fascinated. "And then what?"

"Well, that kind of sobered her up. She covered herself with her arms and ran into the house. Isn't that freaky? I thought people in films were far out, but musicians are really off the wall."

I wasn't sure how much of this was Jenny's usual dramatic embroidery—the girl was behaving in a perfectly normal way at the moment, though she did look a little drawn and weary. In any case, I ignored the elusive suspicion that was buzzing around the fringes of my mind like an audible but invisible fly in a bedroom. I had more urgent concerns.

I told Jenny that I had some personal business to take care of, I'd see her later, and cut across the lawn toward the Music Shed, concentrating on the tasks ahead so that I wouldn't hear the fly buzzing.

8

To ONE SIDE of the backstage area outside the musicians' locker rooms, the table with its coffee urn, paper cups, and plates of bagels and brownies was, as it had been yesterday, the focus of a shifting group of musicians, but the faces and conversations this morning were considerably more somber. No laughter, no imitations of soloists, a very subdued group.

The same young boy I had seen there the day before was still sitting on the same bench next to the table. He had fair hair and freckles and an earnest expression and kept busy, removing used paper cups from the table, mopping up a spill with a paper napkin, checking the sugar and milk.

I saw Shura going into the locker room. I saw Joseph Holchek at a distance, munching on a brownie, standing on the fringe of a group of three musicians in earnest conversation. I walked up to him, affecting, I hoped, the enthusiastic gait of an avid fan.

"Mr. Holchek?"

He turned, his watery blue eyes behind the thick glasses giving me a bleak but not actively hostile look.

"I'm the president of the Sloan's Ford Garden Society," I said, twinkling, and thinking of my six unhealthy begonias and the row of bedraggled baby asters, "and I read in the BSO booklet that you're an amateur horticulturist—"

The eyes looked a little less bleak. He popped the last of the brownie into his mouth and wiped his hands on a paper napkin.

"Most of our members," I continued creatively, "are music lovers, and it would be of tremendous interest to them if I could give a talk on a garden cultivated by one of the first violinists of the Boston Symphony. Would it be a terrible imposition to ask to see your garden?" The part really needed an English accent, a floppy hat, and a chiffon dress.

Holchek cleared his throat. "You would like to see my garden?"

"*Very* much."

"Well—" He tried not to look pleased. "Possible. Possible. This afternoon is no rehearsal. Maybe a half-hour could be arranged. Two o'clock?"

"That would be gr— . . . lovely!"

I took down the address and the directions in between Holchek's warnings that the early summer flowers were finished, the roses were not doing as well as expected, and the herb garden was suffering from the dry spell.

The loudspeaker system came alive, hollowly announcing that it was time to go onstage, and the musicians began to put down their paper cups, swallow the last bit of bagel, step on dropped cigarettes, and move up the stairs into the locker rooms.

The fair-haired, freckled boy behind the coffee urn got up and moved around the table, tidying up, placing the unused cups and uneaten food to one side. I approached him, dropping my impersonation of a lobotomized matron.

"Are you in charge of this operation?" I asked with a friendly smile, indicating the table and its accumulated debris.

He looked up, colored slightly, and said yes, he was. He couldn't have been more than fifteen.

"How'd you get the job?"

"My father's in the orchestra. Every year they give the concession to one of us—one of the kids whose parent's in the orchestra."

"That's great. Looks like you do a good job. How do you work it?"

"Well, I get the coffee from the cafeteria—"

"And the cream and sugar?"

He nodded. "And I make the other stuff."

"You *make* it? At home?"

"Well, I don't make the bagels," he said, admitting inadequacy, "I get those ready-made. I just fill 'em at home. With cream cheese. But I make the brownies."

"You ever make anything special?" I asked. "For instance, if it's someone's birthday? A special brownie with 'Happy Birthday' on it?"

He shrugged. "I guess I could. It hasn't happened yet." He slipped the uneaten bagels into one plastic bag and the brownies into another.

"If you made a study of it," I said, "you'd probably find that certain kinds of musicians tend to like one thing more than another. Flutes always choose brownies, clarinets always eat bagels—?"

He considered. "No. Sometimes they take both."

A lot of help you are.

"But by now," I went on relentlessly, "you must have figured out how many of each you're going to need. You must know who likes what. Don't some of them pick the same thing every day?"

The boy was beginning to look at me as though I'd made an early start on senility.

"It's hard to say," he mumbled, "I just figure on a certain amount and I usually just have a couple left over."

I searched desperately for a graceful way of extracting the information, and found none. I settled for, "I suppose your testimony will be very important after what happened to Mr. Damaskin."

He looked startled, and it occurred to me, belatedly, that he wouldn't necessarily know about the poison. The police might not yet have gotten around to him. "I mean, since they don't know why he died, they'll probably want to know what he was doing at various times, and if he looked ill and so on."

He answered with the one word I didn't want to hear.
"Why?"

I looked at this fifteen-year-old and tried to remember
what my own boys would have responded to at that age.
Television immediately came to mind.

"It's routine procedure," I said.

That he understood.

"Well, yesterday at the break he looked okay, talking and
everything."

"Helping himself to coffee and bagel—"

He looked defensive. "So did everybody else, and they
didn't get sick."

"I guess he must have been feeling all right then. If not,
he probably would have sat down and asked someone else
to get his coffee for him."

"Well, he didn't. He came right up and took it himself.
He even made a joke that I was skimping on the cream
cheese so I could make a bigger profit."

Another, older boy appeared, and my fair-haired lad,
looking relieved, turned away and began a muttered conversation with him.

As I went off across the lawn toward the Lion's Gate, I
could hear the orchestra tuning up, and I thought of
Greenfield settling into his seat for a comfortable two and a
half hours of what he claimed would be "observation of the
orchestra," while he sent me around, in 90 percent humidity,
to a series of sticky confrontations. I felt a certain kinship
with the gladiator in the wings watching the nobility up
there in their box with a bunch of grapes.

I got into the car and took off for Lenox. The wheel was
slippery with moisture-laden air and my lightweight jeans
weighed a ton. I hadn't expected to stay in the Berkshires
through several changes of weather. Clothes were going to
be a problem. I'd have to pick up a thin cotton something to
wear.

Before long I found myself approaching the house into
which I'd been instructed to maneuver my way. There was
no sign of activity anywhere on the street and that was no

surprise in this heat. Two cars stood in front of the Damaskins' house, one in the driveway and one at the curb. Farther up there was a police car in front of the Charnovs'.
God, yes, the police would be questioning Nadia. Little did
they know what they were in for.

I slowed dramatically and crawled along the curb, just in
case old gimlet-eyes was watching through a shuttered window, the way those blowsy women with the gin bottles do in
certain movies. I turned off the ignition, rolled to a stop,
started up again, gunning the engine with a roar, and
quickly let up on the accelerator so that it would die, as it so
often had when I didn't want it to. Then I got out, looking
worried.

I hurried around to the front of the car, released the hood,
and stood there helplessly, doing an imitation of Eleanor
Springer. It wasn't brilliant, but I firmly believe that all experience should be put to practical use whenever possible.

I poked ineffectually at the black greasy coils and pieces
of metal under the hood, looked anxiously up and down the
street, and hoped it would not be the wrong person who
came to my aid. I needn't have worried. *No* one came to my
aid. There wasn't the slightest sign that my performance
had been witnessed. I could have stripped and come up the
street on a horse without causing a single craning of the
neck.

I went around to the hatchback door, opened it, rooted in
the corner, and came up with a tire iron and a jack. I put the
jack on the ground, lifted my right arm and threw the tire
iron, with all the force I could muster, onto the jack. The resultant clang of metal echoed up and down the road. If that
doesn't do it, I thought—and the door opened, and Mr.
Avery, tall and skinny and suspicious as a miser at a gathering of poor relations, stood in the opening.

I pretended not to see him, struggled mightily putting the
jack and tire iron back in the Honda, went around to the
open hood, mopping my brow piteously with a handkerchief, let my shoulders slump, my head droop, and my arms

hang limply. I did everything but don sandwich-boards announcing Damsel in Distress.

He came halfway down the walk.

"What's all that noise about?" he demanded.

I turned quickly, trying to look startled. "Oh, I'm *so* sorry. I dropped the—I was trying to find something to fix the—there seems to be something wrong with my car. It was making peculiar noises and then it died, and I can't get it started again. I've got plenty of gas so it's not that. I think it was heating up. I'm afraid I'm not very good with engines. Could you recommend some garage in town—?"

He took his time answering. His little eyes glittered while the heat glued my jeans to my legs.

"You could try McTeague," he admitted grudgingly, "probably knows as much as any of them."

"McTeague. Thank you." I looked around as though confidently expecting to find the country road lined with public telephone kiosks. "Oh—uh—would it be too much trouble if I used your phone?"

This took even longer. He eyed me carefully, looking for hidden weapons, babies, or encyclopedias. Finally, he made an abrupt gesture toward the house and started back in.

"This is very good of you," I said, saving myself from being struck by the screen door as he went through ahead of me without holding it.

The house was small, dark, and stuffy, the cheap blinds drawn on all the windows, the musty furniture dating from the thirties. He pointed to the telephone on a spindly tiered table attached to a standing lamp. On one of the tiers was a telephone book and I looked up McTeague's number, turned so that my back stood between Mr. Avery and his telephone, dialed the number, and put my finger on the receiver rest.

I told the dead telephone who and where I was and why I was calling and asked it please to send someone as soon as possible, then I sighed deeply and put my hand to my head.

"I hate to impose," I said weakly, "but I feel a little dizzy.

It must be the heat. Would you mind very much if I splashed a little cold water on my face?"

He backed away from me indignantly, as though I had forced my way into his home under the false pretense of being a healthy person, only to drop my burden of serious illness on his unsuspecting shoulders the minute I'd gained access. However, he finally grunted and led me down a murky green hallway. I had a bad moment when I realized he was heading for the kitchen, but fortunately caught a glimpse of what I was after through a half-open door and said, "This will do fine, thank you," and stepped in and shut the door.

I've been in many a bathroom in my time, both public and private, but this was the first one for which the only adjective was pathetic. One thin, worn towel in a faded plaid pattern hung grayly over an aluminum rod. The floor linoleum of curdled blue and dusty red swirls was worn and curling at the edges, the toilet seat was chipped and the shower curtain, sprinkled with glutinous-looking fish and hanging over an old-fashioned tub, had come off some of its loops and been repaired with Scotch tape.

I suddenly felt great pity for this lonely old man living frugally amid his scraps and patches and deprived now even of his one living companion, unattractive though he'd been. I could even understand his animosity toward his sleek, well-fed neighbors.

On the other hand, there were plenty of poor and lonely old men who were not mean-spirited and vindictive. And if he was guilty of more than that . . .

I ran the water loudly in the stained sink and quickly opened the door of the medicine cabinet above it. Band-Aids, cough medicine, aerosol shaving cream, various ointments and prescription bottles, laxatives, aspirin—the usual. I memorized a name, shut the cabinet door, splashed water on my face, took a tissue from my bag, and emerged dabbing at my cheeks.

Avery was standing guard at the end of the hallway.

"That really helped," I said and went determinedly back into the living room. "If I could just sit for a minute—"

Before he could stop me I collapsed into an unyielding armchair.

"This is a very cozy little house. Your wife is obviously a good housekeeper."

"My wife's been dead for twenty years," he snapped.

"Oh, I'm sorry. And you live here all alone?"

The crevices bracketing his thin mouth deepened. "All alone now, all right, thanks to that murdering swine next door."

"You mean"—I registered horror—"someone *killed* your wife?"

"My dog. Killed him in cold blood."

"Oh no!"

"Ran him over. Never gave him a chance."

"How awful! But—couldn't it have been an accident?"

"Wasn't any accident. Rotten swine was out to get my dog, no two ways about it. Got no satisfaction from the police, neither. Said I couldn't prove it. Cold-blooded murderer woulda got away scot-free if it was left to the police."

"What did happen?"

An expression of malicious satisfaction tightened his mouth. "Won't kill any more dogs, that's certain. Dropped dead."

I swallowed, with difficulty. Vindication was a mild word for it.

"I have a dog at home and I know just how you feel." Mentally I apologized to George for coupling him with Avery's foul-tempered animal.

Avery merely nodded grimly seven or eight times.

"And a neighbor, too," I said. "I always think that's so sad, after people have been living side by side for years, getting to be almost like family, walking in and out of each other's houses—"

"I don't walk in and out of anybody's house but my own," Mr. Avery said acidly, "and I thank everybody else to do the same."

"Still, it's so much worse when a terrible thing like this is done by someone so close by. Someone you can see from your window any hour of the day or night. Imagine having to see him sitting at breakfast, or out on his patio preparing a barbecue—you can probably smell his steak grilling from here, or his coffee in the morning—" I had moved unobtrusively toward a window on the side of the house facing the Damaskins', and now I moved the blind aside to look out. There was a border marking the boundary of Avery's property sharply defined by a picket fence—I could only surmise he couldn't afford a ten-foot wall topped by broken glass—which gave way, at the back of the house, to a line of thick bushes, through which even a mildly determined individual could scamper quickly enough to make it to the rear of the Damaskins' house and back in under a minute.

But Avery had either decided he'd used up his communication quota for the day, or become suspicious at my rapid recovery from the "dizzy spell." He pulled the blind back over the window and clomped uncompromisingly to the front door.

"Mechanic should be along any minute," he said. "Better get out there to flag him down."

His hospitality was boundless. I thanked him again and went back to the car, wondering how long I would have to stand there in the heat while he watched from behind the screen door. It must have been minutes but seemed hours that I stood there peering anxiously up and down the road and then at my watch, and occasionally bending over the open hood. Finally I pantomimed disgust, went around to the driver's seat, turned the key in the ignition and allowed it to sputter out twice, then finally let it catch. I rushed out to shut the hood, looked up and down the road once more for good measure, and took off, leaving Avery to conclude I had gone straight for McTeague's to forestall the mechanic.

Actually I drove up the road only a mile or so, turned around, and headed back down the street in accordance with my projected itinerary. I had a distinct feeling, however, that this was not the time to carry out the next item on the agenda. My original plan, to park on the far side of the Charnovs' and make my way through Nadia's patio and across through the trees onto the Damaskins' property, thus avoiding being seen by Avery, had lost some of its appeal in light of the fact that the police car still sat in Nadia's drive-way.

I decided my "condolence call" would have to wait—it was not, in any case, a prospect which fired me with enthu-siasm—and I was about to speed on toward Lenox when I saw a woman come down to the street from the Damaskins' house and get into the Chevy at the curb. She was a short, square, sturdy woman wearing flat crepe-soled shoes and carrying a plastic handbag. She had the slightly arrogant look of a hospital nurse, the slightly aggressive attitude of a seamstress who thinks her work is being criticized, the no-nonsense walk of an efficient waitress, and that refusal to be intimidated that is the hallmark of a salesgirl accustomed to catering to rich customers. Put them all together they spell cleaning woman. Luck was with me.

I slowed to let her swing out from the curb and make a U-turn, and I followed her into town.

She parked on a side street and I did the same. She walked up the street and into a supermarket, and I caught up with her as she was considering a cabbage.

"Excuse me—I was driving by the Damaskins' house when you came out. I just wanted to ask how Mrs. Damas-kin is getting along."

She looked up at me, tucking her double chin into her neck and examining me from behind pink-framed glasses with her sharp green eyes.

"Wouldn't expect her to be dancing on the tabletop, would you," she said. "She was sleeping, as a matter of fact. Why didn't you go up to the house?"

"I've only met her once. I was just wondering if there was anything I could do to help."

"Not much anybody can do," she said, dropping the cab-bage into her cart and eyeing a bag of onions. "What's done is done. If I'd known what was coming I'd never've gone there to work yesterday. I don't enjoy getting told off for doing what I was hired to do in the first place. That sister of hers—!"

I picked up a peach. Eleanor had made a good guess. They were small and hard.

"I suppose," I said, "you have to make allowances for the things people say under those conditions."

She snorted. "*I* don't have to make allowances. I have as much sympathy as the next person, and I've never had anything against Mrs. D., we got along fine and I feel sorry for her. But that sister! 'If only you hadn't polished the furniture!' she says, 'if only you hadn't touched the bottles!' If that's her idea of cleaning, I wouldn't want to live in *her* house." She marched off to the meat counter and I followed.

"Do you work for Mrs. Damaskin every day?"

"One day a week. I only dropped in today to see if she needed anything. One day a week and it had to happen *that* day. The luck of the Irish." She deliberated between pork chops and neck of lamb.

"So you saw Mr. Damaskin yesterday—?"

"He rushed in and out again, if that's what you mean. Didn't seem very sick to me. Came in from rehearsal, grabbed his tennis things, ran out again. She'd left him a shrimp salad in the fridge before she took off to visit their boy at camp, but he didn't even touch it. Came back again about four o'clock, ran in and out of the shower and off to rehearsal again. Not so much as a glass of water. So if it was anything he ate or drank, it wasn't in *that* house. At least not between nine and five." She chose the pork chops and started for the checkout counter. I suddenly remembered something.

"What kind of bottles?" I asked as she deposited her purchases on the counter.

She looked blank.

"The bottles she said you shouldn't have touched."

She gave me a speculative look, then a short laugh. "Scotch. Wine. Brandy."

"Vodka?"

"Nope. No vodka. Anyway, he didn't have any of that, I can swear to it. Those bottles were under my eye both times he was there." With a small tight smile she added, "As I told the police."

She paid for her groceries and we left the store, and outside on the sidewalk she said "Bye-bye" quite dismissively, and trotted off.

I went in the opposite direction, looking for a drugstore. The street was thick with window-shoppers ogling the antique shops and boutiques and spacious, gracious white-painted homes now doing service as guest houses and restaurants: New York and Boston ladies in their Calvin Klein pants, kids in cut-off jeans and limp Indian shirts, locals in their print dresses or shirtsleeves, with their Norman Rockwell faces . . . how delightful it would have been, I thought, to stroll around with nothing to do but look. . . .

I found a drugstore. No Cutter's. I found a clothes shop and bought a thin cotton wraparound skirt, which I wore, gratefully, giving the clerk my jeans to wrap up. I looked at my watch, ran back to the car, and drove at a pretty good clip back to Tanglewood.

I found Greenfield waiting, as scheduled, on the porch of the Main House. The rehearsal had not been over for more than ten minutes and he could not have been standing there for more than six, but the look of exhaustion and reproach in his eyes suggested I had kept him waiting for days in some remote and shelterless mountain pass.

"I was about," he said, "to send out a search party."

"Private investigation cannot punch a clock. The drugstore had no Cutter's. I could get you something else."

"Try another store." He started off the porch.

"Why don't we lunch here?" I said, realizing I was parched and hungry.

He cast a speculative eye toward the cafeteria. "Not if we want to talk."

"We could get something and carry it out to a tree far from the madding crowd."

"Sit on the ground?"

"Thoreau recommends it."

"There are several ways of interpreting Thoreau," he said, scratching at his arm. "Based on personal experience, the joys of close bodily contact with nature are largely imagined. Usually by someone caught in midtown traffic during Christmas week." He left the porch and started down the path to the gate.

I glanced at the large bulletin board, thinking of Jenny's story about the Botticelli girl, Allison. All the notices I'd seen the day before were still there, with one exception. In the lower right hand corner there was an empty rectangle. The corner where I'd seen that cryptic note, "N. SAME TIME SAME PLACE. A." I went down the path after Greenfield.

A for Allison?

N for—?

No. Surely not. The girl was young enough to be his—oh, come off it, Maggie. These days it wouldn't even rate a PG.

I thought of that first night on the Charnovs' patio and Damaskin confirming that Shura would see Fran home from the dinner party because he had to coach a student chamber group.

Could the chamber group possibly consist of one golden-haired girl?

Was it possible Fran suspected? Or *knew*?

"Maggie."

I stopped walking and turned around. Greenfield was standing patiently by the Honda, past which I had walked some twenty feet.

9

"So THERE it is," I concluded over fruit salad and cottage cheese. "I have garnered nothing but negatives. Damaskin did not obligingly receive either food or drink from anyone else's hands at the coffee break, and he ate the same food and drank the same coffee as anyone else. He did not, according to the waitresses, have lunch here. He did go into the bar, and Irene says she poured a glass of tomato juice for him, but she had just poured three others from the same pitcher and they were for those three old people who are staying here and they seem to be more or less alive. At home, if you believe the cleaning woman—and they watch *everything*—he neither consumed nor imbibed, and in fact didn't have *time* to, so it appears the man went from eleven to five without ingesting anything but some innocuous tomato juice." I swallowed a piece of peach and remembered something. "Unless—"

There was a considerable pause. Greenfield sat with head bent over his tuna fish, his fork poised and his eyes searching my face from under his scraggy brows.

"No," I said, "forget it."

He slowly lowered his fork and sat up.

"There are two actions," he said, "that are almost equally reprehensible to me. One is the act of beginning a sentence and then refusing to finish it. The other is murder."

"You won't like it—"

"Irrelevant."

"All right. The cleaning woman was talking about the whisky and wine bottles at the Damaskins'. She didn't mention vodka. I asked about it. She said, 'Nope, no vodka.' If you remember, they borrowed a bottle of vodka from Nadia the night before. It occurred to me that the vodka might have been hidden in the Damaskins' bedroom, and Noel might have taken a drink from it there, which would account for the cleaning woman's not knowing about it."

"Why should it be hidden?"

I shrugged. "I had a woman working for me once who went through sherry the way a kid goes through popcorn. Elliot finally hid the sherry in the piano bench whenever she came."

"And?"

"And—" I took a long time swallowing a piece of lettuce. "And there are only four people who knew it was in that house." I lowered my eyes and wished I could leave the table. Several months went by. I did not look up to see what color Greenfield's face had become.

"I won't honor that," he said finally in a voice that was deadly calm, "even with a comment."

I had no intention of reminding him that only one thing about the human animal is certain.

We finished our salads in silence and when eventually I managed to raise my eyes he seemed to be a fairly ordinary color.

"About Avery," he said, "you didn't give me the name of the drugstore he used."

"It's in Pittsfield," I said.

"Pittsfield," he murmured. "Why would anyone within five minutes of Lenox use a drugstore in Pittsfield . . ."

"Because the name of the drugstore is Avery's."

He regarded me with a look that could almost be described as fond.

"Avery's." He all but crooned the word. And then went back to his more normal state of depression. "Not that it eliminates the problem. If the intended victim doesn't partake of the substance with the poison in it, the poison isn't

going to poison him. Even assuming Damaskin drank vodka
in his bedroom, which is highly unlikely, Avery didn't know
about the vodka. The vodka wasn't visible. And Damaskin
didn't touch anything else in that house." He thought for a
minute. "Find out if he took pills. Hayfever, vitamins, iron
pills—even aspirin, if he took it regularly." He sighed,
reached into his shirt pocket, and produced a folded yellow
sheet of paper, which he unfolded and handed to me. I recognized Greenfield's inimitable scrawl. At the top of the
page was a limerick.

"Sir Beecham rehearsed four bars *of* it,
Said, "Well, men, I think you're *above* it,"
Said the flute, "What, no more? I've not played it before!"
Said Beecham, "Oh you're going to *love* it!"

Below that, a game of tic-tac-toe. Further down, the figure
43,875 divided by .40, and a lot of other numbers either
being added to, subtracted from, or multiplying one another. A few doodles. Below that, an attempt to make an an-
agram of the name *Jan Sorrel,* which resulted only in
"Jason" and "Ansel," and at the bottom a G-clef with the
notes F♯, E, D, and C circled, with the circle not quite including all of the F♯.

I raised my inquiring eyebrows at Greenfield.

"Before rehearsal," Greenfield said, "I got Shura to take
me backstage and show me around. One of the things I saw
was the music library. Two small, cluttered rooms. I was introduced to the principal librarian, a civilized man. Music
parts in folders were filed on shelves in the inner room, a
separate folder, marked, for each stand. The parts are transported to and from the stage on a cart, a kind of primitive
green bookcase on wheels. Apparently, in the aftermath of
last night's disconcerting events, the parts for the Ravel, al-
though collected from the stands, had not been replaced on
the shelves; they were still on the cart. While I was there
the librarian removed them and placed them temporarily on
a table nearby, only a step from the door, put the music for
this morning's rehearsal on the cart, and trundled it off.

"I asked for the men's room, and told Shura I'd meet him

outside. When he was gone, I went back into the library, located the music for Damaskin's stand, tucked it under my shirt, went back to the men's room, copied that—" he gestured to the yellow sheet, "and went back to the library with the music under my shirt. Unfortunately, there were people going in and out of the office. I had to wait around. Someone asked if they could help me. It was all very precarious and uncomfortable, but there was no other way to get a look at it without having to answer a lot of unanswerable questions. I finally replaced it and I don't think anyone noticed me. What you see there, with the exception of the musical notes, was on the inside of the folder, and it's probably not relevant, though you never know. The notes F-sharp, E, D, and C-sharp were circled on the music itself. What does it suggest to you?"

"Those are the first four notes of the *Rapsodie Espagnole.*"

"They're the *same* as the first four notes. That motif is repeated several times. These notes were circled at the point in the music where Damaskin collapsed. That was the note he was making before he collapsed. Whatever it means."

"F-sharp, E, D, C-sharp." I stared at the letters. They meant nothing. I could hear them in my head, hear that soft, misty sound, but they didn't translate into a code I could decipher.

"Obviously," Greenfield said, "it's as crystal clear to you as it is to me." He took the yellow sheet from my hand, folded it, and put it back in his pocket. "You'd better go, you'll be late for your appointment with Mr. Holchek."

He stood up, dropped his napkin by his plate, and left the terrace table where he had persuaded the waitress to serve us so that we wouldn't be overheard.

I drank down the last of my iced coffee, checked that I still had Mr. Holchek's directions in my pocket, and went off, with the sound of F-sharp, E, D, C-sharp repeating endlessly in my head. Coming out of Wheatleigh Drive, I turned left toward Stockbridge.

The house was on a side road off Route 7, a cottage of

weathered cedar shingles, standing far back from the road behind a quarter-acre of highly cultivated garden.

There was no grass except what was necessary to walk on between the fragrant beds of eye-catching colors. A thick, four-foot-high privet hedge backed by a wire-mesh fence ran around the perimeter with a gate where the brick walk to the house met the road. I'd left the car on the cinder parking area to one side where a dark green Ford was standing and was barely through the gate when the cottage door opened and Mr. Holchek, eyeglasses and bald dome glinting in the sun, came down to meet me. He was carrying a kind of canvas pith helmet, which he clapped onto his head before greeting me in his brusque, unsmiling fashion.

I gave him my lavish, garden-club smile.

"So," he said, "if you are president of a garden club, you know something about horticulture. You will recognize what I have here."

"Well," I faltered, "we're all amateurs, of course. The club is only a year old. But we're learning all the time."

"There is a great deal to learn. Unfortunate you are missing the baby-blue-eyes, the Dutch iris, Canterbury bells, larkspur, all gone. In the spring they cover all of this corner. Also this—" he pointed to a drift of rich blue flowers bordering a small carpet of pink and red, "Chinese forget-me-not, and the red, you know what that is—?"

"Uh—"

"Candy tuft they call it. Almost past the bloom now. In June they are best. Over here, calendula"—I looked carefully but saw only a large bed of green leaves—"in the spring and fall you have flowers so big"—he indicated a small hand-span —"a color like apricots. The leaves you can cook for a vegetable."

We went on, and I oohed and aahed and made notes as we examined masses of marigolds, rivers of red and violet petunias, glowing orange-gold California poppies, purple ageratum, pastel verbenas, gazania like yellow stars, tall cosmos—their pink, magenta, and lavender daisy-heads nodding on the ends of frail, five-foot stems, borders of pinky-orange salpiglossis and blue lobelia, African daisies, zinnias in the bold, vivid colors of a Van Gogh palette, a cascade of small yellow and white mignonette scenting the air with a sweet, clean fragrance, cream-colored nasturtium—

"You know, of course," said Mr. Holchek, leaning over to twitch off a dead leaf, "that in nasturtium also the leaves and flowers are good to eat, like watercress."

This I happened to know, and I also knew something else, something I'd been hoping to be able to use as an introduction to less-horticultural conversation.

"But the seeds," I said, "I've heard are poisonous."

Immediately the serene concentration with which he was regarding his handiwork was replaced by a quivering of the jowls and a total disappearance of the thin lips. Then he muttered, "True, you must be careful," and moved on to the rose garden, discoursing on soil composition, optimum planting times, conditions of climate that affected the need for direct or indirect sunlight, the hazards inflicted by various garden pests, the advisability of transplanting—I thought I'd lost my one opportunity, and wondered how on earth I was going to make the transition from a moisture level to a dead violinist, when I caught sight of a stand of tubular purple flowers with large wooly leaves. I knew what they were.

"What beautiful foxglove!" I said. "Aren't they the ones that produce digitalis?"

This time he looked at me steadily. "You are very concerned with toxic properties."

"Well," I improvised hastily, "we had an herbilist down to speak to us last month, and she talked about edible plants and dangerous plants and she mentioned foxglove and nasturtium and—ah—" I searched wildly through my very limited compendium of miscellaneous knowledge. "She told us that herbs were once widely used for medicinal purposes. To ward off the plague, for instance. She said the judges in the English courts still keep bunches of dried herbs on their benches to protect them from diseases brought in by the criminals."

"Criminals," he repeated, and turned the back of his thick shoulders to me and trudged ahead to the next display. "So criminals are automatically contaminated." There was no particular edge to his voice but for a moment my pulse quickened. Was his response a normal expression of a liberal view, or was he identifying with the wrong side of the law? "Well, of course, the practice began a very long time ago," I apologized, "in England. Where they have so many benevolent as well as poisonous—"

"You would like to see English herbs? I have many of them here. Also English field flowers. In this part of the country are all the flowers you find in Shakespeare—a lady wrote about this in the Berkshire newspaper—" He pointed ahead to a delightful tangle of wild and cultivated flowers. "Some already gone for the season. I do nothing for them, only the columbine I cultivate. The rest are a gift from nature. Flowers from *King Lear* and *Hamlet*, *A Midsummer Night's Dream*—all here—primrose, cowslip, buttercup, violet, daisy—from my garden you could make a wreath for Ophelia's hair."

Or a poison for somebody's heart?

Suddenly he bent over and gently broke a stalk of exquisite columbine and gave it to me, not looking at me, embarrassed, clomping off to the herb garden, an aging man with a passion for lovely growing things. I wanted to pack it all up and go back to Greenfield and tell him I was not cut out for the job.

Then I reminded myself of all the murderers whose virtues were legend. I reminded myself that *someone* was threatening the other members of the BSO and that one of those was Shura. I went on to look at the herb garden at the back of his house.

"These also you find in Shakespeare," he said, showing me thyme and lavender, comfrey and fennel, marjoram, rosemary and rue.

Shakespeare, I thought, was inescapable. Shakespeare in a book at Wheatleigh, Shakespeare in the music at Tangle-

wood. And now Shakespeare in the garden. Would any
writer ever again so permeate the fabric of our existence?

We had made a complete tour of Mr. Holchek's grounds
and stood now by a back porch decorated with hanging bas-
kets of black-eyed susan vine, the deep orange flowers with
their dark purple centers dripping luxuriantly over some old
canvas deck chairs.

I made my thank you speech and he waved it away. "My
wife," he said, "prepared some iced tea before she went to
the post office. Excuse me. Sit in the shade." He gestured
brusquely to a deck chair. "The sun is too strong today." He
went through a screen door and soon returned with a tray
containing pitcher and glasses. I had been preparing my
segue to the matter I still had to broach, and I tried it out as
I accepted a glass of iced tea.

"I'm sorry," I said, "that I upset you before, talking about
digitalis. I wasn't thinking. It was very thoughtless of me,
after what happened to your partner."

"My *partner?*"

"The man who sat next to you in the orchestra. I was at
the rehearsal when he collapsed."

Mr. Holchek was not too sentimental, even for my benefit,
about the late Noel Damaskin.

"We all die," he said impatiently, clinking the ice cubes in
his glass.

"Such a young man—"

He turned on me. "Is it better for old people to die? You
think it's easier to face death because you have lived a
longer time? You think old people are not so important as
younger people? Will not be missed? Have nothing to give
the world?"

"Not at all. I—"

"I have known old orchestra musicians who were a *hundred* times better than the young ones! Experience—" He
choked, coughed, resumed with quivering jowls, "Maturity
—comprehension! What can you comprehend at twenty? At
forty? Nothing! You think you would get those performances with an orchestra full of kids? You think energy is ev-

erything? Technique is everything? There is more to music than beating time!"

"I'm sure that—"

"They are so anxious—so anxious to get us out of the way —to push us off the chair and move up! Ambition—that's all they think about, not music. Ambition!" He pushed himself out of the deck chair. "I have some business to take care of now—"

"Oh, of course." I got up. "I appreciate your giving me so much time. Really, it's been wonderful. A beautiful garden. Just lovely. I can't wait to tell the club about it!"

He nodded, unsmiling, and led me around to the front of the house.

I had the feeling, as I got into the car, waving to him gaily, that he wasn't entirely convinced I was the simple soul I pretended to be. I wondered if he remembered seeing me in the backstage area with Shura, and if he would ask him about me.

I turned right at the Red Lion, parked on the main street, and sought out a drugstore. No Cutter's. Everything but. I bought some toothpaste, went back to the car, and drove along the main street and Route 7 to Lenox. I could no longer put off the Fran Damaskin business and I dreaded it.

When I reached the too-familiar road, I sped past Avery's, parked just beyond the Charnovs' house, and made my way, as I had planned to do earlier, through Nadia's back patio and the adjacent trees, to the Damaskins' property. There were no police cars about, and if Nadia was at home she gave no evidence of having seen me. She would not have presented a problem, but I was just as happy for one less confrontation.

A tall woman, built like a fullback with a pompadour of gray-streaked brown hair, opened the door to my tentative knock. She was reluctant to let me in, but I said I was leaving town and just wanted to convey my sympathy, and she finally stood aside for me to pass, with a lot of fussy gestures and audible misgivings about whether her sister should be subjected to more visitors at this time.

I walked into an air-conditioned room thick with expensive contemporary furnishings in the midst of which stood a Mason and Hamlin baby grand, its closed top covered with silver-framed photographs of Noel Damaskin showing his teeth in company with a variety of celebrities from Arthur Ashe to Efrem Zimbalist. Fran was resting limply against an assortment of woven cushions, wearing a patterned cotton Chinese robe, her feet up on a square upholstered hassock. Her cheeks were hollow, her eyes half-shut, her lips dry and slightly cracked, and her expression vacant. She didn't seem to know who I was. I reminded her.

"Oh yes," she said hoarsely, "yes. Thank you for coming." Her eyes wandered vaguely to the French doors through which I caught a glimpse of the back of Avery's house.

"It seems incredible," I said. "I'd seen him, you know, just hours before, swimming in the pool at Wheatleigh."

Her eyes returned to me then. "At Wheatleigh," she said, "yes, of course, he would go to Wheatleigh."

"He was playing tennis with Mr. Sorrel."

"With Sorrel. Oh. That too."

That *too?* I felt a flutter of apprehension.

"Don't you think you should rest now, Fran?" the sister fussed.

"That's all I've been doing," she said wearily.

"He seemed fine when I saw him," I said. Not true. I remembered his face as he came down from the second floor.

"He wasn't sick," she said slowly, "he was never sick. He didn't know what it was to be ill. He made fun of me because I took so many pills. . . . He never took a pill in his life . . . not even an aspirin. . . . He said pills could do you more harm than good . . . they all have side effects, he said, they're poison . . . Poison."

"Now Fran," the sister said, fussing with the cushions, "don't dwell on it."

"Have they—uh—have they been able to find the source of —of whatever it was that—?"

"I really think she should get her mind off it," the sister snapped.

"Iris," Fran said, "is there any tea?"

"I'll make some." She went off, but not without a cautionary glance at me.

"They haven't been able to trace it?" I asked when the sister was out of the room.

"No. No, they don't know how, or where—"

"Did you have any visitors the day before?"

She wrinkled her forehead slightly, as though the effort of trying to remember was painful. "No," she said, "no, the . . . the police asked me that. There was . . . there was no one here."

I heard the tinkle of cup against saucer in the kitchen, and then the sound of voices. Fran closed her eyes. A boy came into the room. He looked about fourteen, thin, with a foxy face and a sullen expression. He had none of Noel Damaskin's characteristics except the gray eyes.

"I want to go back to camp and get my bike," he said, "and Iris won't take me."

"Maybe tomorrow," his mother said without opening her eyes.

"Bobby!" Iris hissed, coming in bearing a dainty cup and saucer in her large, awkward hands, "I told you not to bother her!"

Bobby gave her a venomous look and went out of the house.

Iris shook her head and placed a coaster on the glass table at Fran's elbow and the cup of tea on the coaster.

"She hasn't eaten anything solid," she whispered ominously, "since it happened."

A telephone rang in another room and Iris disappeared.

"Fran," I said quietly, "when I was talking about the tennis game with Mr. Sorrel, you said 'That, too.' What did you—"

Her mouth had fallen slightly open and her chest rose and fell gently. She was asleep. In the other room I could hear Iris in funereal tones carrying on what promised to be a lengthy conversation. I went down a hallway quietly, hoping the telephone was not in the bedroom. It wasn't; the voice came from the kitchen. Through an open doorway I caught sight of a corner of opulent green silk bedspread and I went in and found the adjoining bathroom. Lush and sparkling, with burgundy towels as thick as quilts, sink fittings of antique gold, and a faint scent of Yves St. Laurent aftershave. A far cry from Mr. Avery across the way. The medicine cabinet contained hairspray, nail polish, hand cream, eye cream, throat cream, suntan lotion, body lotion, bath powder, deodorant, shampoo, and an assortment of prescription pills all labeled with Fran's name. I flushed the toilet just in case Iris should be in the vicinity and went back to the bedroom. Abstract prints on the walls, a dressing table crowded with perfume bottles and the results of Revlon's research, a series of louvered wardrobe doors covering one wall, one pair with a lock from which a key stuck out. There was no point in looking for vodka; if it had been here the police would have it by now.

I left the bedroom. Iris was still on the phone in the kitchen. I went to the front door and out into the heat. Bobby was tossing a basketball at—but not through—a loop above the garage door.

"Bobby," I said, "have you ever been to Wheatleigh?"

He looked at me and I was reminded of the solitary smugness of the rich kid in the "Our Gang" series.

"What's Wheatleigh?" he demanded.

"A very fancy place near Tanglewood. A kind of palace. I thought your father might have taken you there at some time."

"The only place he ever took me was to Friendly's in Great Barrington for a soda." He went back to tossing the ball. I went around the side of the house, across Nadia's patio, and back to the car. It would be almost five by the time I got back to Wheatleigh, and I felt like the inside of a jogging suit after a long hard run, the air wrapping me like a hot wet blanket, from the damp hair at the nape of my neck to the burning soles of my feet.

As I drove, a large purplish cloud passed between earth and sun, and the relief was instant, but brief. The sun came out again.

I parked the car in its usual place opposite the tower, took my wilting columbine and my toothpaste from the dashboard, and poured myself out the door.

"Hi there!"

I didn't have to turn to know who it was, but I turned. Mr. Felker was coming down the cracked stone steps from the tower, the stub of a cigar between his fingers.

"Been to the Garden Center?" he asked.

"No—"

"We saw some flowers like that at the Berkshire Garden Center. Beautiful gardens, roses the size of salad bowls. Hot, isn't it. This is no day to go sightseeing. You should have stayed at the pool. Where did you go?"

"Uh—just to the drugstore." I moved toward the garden and the front portico, hoping to lose him, but he followed.

"In Stockbridge? That's a nice little store. I always visit the drugstores, whatever town we're in. My wife gets tired of it, but it's important to me. I'm in pharmaceutical supplies."

"Mm." I heard a voice from the direction of the front steps call "Mr. Sorrel!" and when I reached the portico Sorrel was standing with one hand on the open door of his apartment and the beard was springing toward him from the front of the house.

"I think we found something that belongs to you," the beard was saying. "One of the gardeners found it, when he was mowing the lawn. It was caught in a bush." He handed Sorrel a small white cardboard rectangle and Sorrel looked at it, thanked him, and went into his rooms, and the beard grinned at me.

"You ought to get down to the pool," Felker was saying, "and cool off."

"I intend to. Excuse me." I caught up with the beard as he went toward the porte cochere. "I'll bet," I said to him, "that was the thing Mr. Sorrel was looking for the other night. I heard him from my window. Where did they find it?"

"Around the side. Not far from where your room is."

"What was it? I'm dying of curiosity."

"Just one of those appointment cards you get in a doctor's office."

"Oh, a doctor's office. Is that all?" I said airily, "The way he was carrying on you'd have thought it was gold bullion." We went into the Hall, where it was fractionally cooler. My mind was darting around among possibilities, like a crazed hummingbird. "But those cards," I said, "don't usually have the patient's name on them. How did you know it was his?"

"There was some writing on the back about BSO rehearsal dates. The boss said it looked like Mr. Sorrel's handwriting. Mr. Greenfield just went to his room if you're looking for him."

"Thanks." I smiled at him; he was an invaluable asset. If I could have thought of any logical excuse for the question, I would have asked if he remembered the doctor's name. But I knew two things about the beard: He was intensely curious and he had a great need to communicate. Any excessive interest in the details of that card and he might easily, and for no malicious reason, convey that interest to Sorrel himself.

I went down the corridor to Greenfield's room, now known as Sloppy Joe's. The pristine white bedspread was covered with scribbled yellow sheets; books and newspapers desecrated the elegant mantel and the wicker chair, an open map drooped over one of the French lingerie chests, on the other chest a cardboard rectangle taken from a laundered shirt was propped against the wall, with F♯, E, D, C♯ written largely across it, and Greenfield himself, in a rumpled T-shirt with his gray locks pointing in several different directions, had a smudge of ink just over his left eyebrow. Sloan's Ford had come to the Raffles Hotel.

"Sorry," I said, "no Cutter's. I tried." I handed him the columbine and he regarded it as though it were a specimen from some unpleasant river bottom.

"From Holchek's garden. I have a lot to tell you."

We went out to the balcony and he sprawled in the big rustic chair and stared at the table, his chin supported by the palm of his hand, as I gave him an account of what I'd learned. It was a respectable haul and I looked forward to some moderate sign of enthusiasm, but not even the discovery that the Damaskins had a closet they could lock seemed to bring a gleam to his eye.

What he finally said was, "What with Holchek's foxglove, Mrs. Damaskin's pills, Avery's family drugstore, Sorrel's doctor's appointment, and Damaskin's refusal to provide us with his consumption of any substance, liquid or solid, into which poison might have been introduced, all we have—" he sighed prodigiously—"is a plethora of possible means and a nullity of method."

10

AN HOUR later, after a quick swim in the pool, a shower, and a change of clothes, I joined Greenfield on the terrace to await the arrival of Shura and Nadia for an early dinner before the concert.

He looked clean and cool in a fresh blue shirt and ice-cream-suit trousers, and he was sitting at a table in the shade of the umbrella. Beside him, with a newspaper in his left hand and his right hand bandaged, was Isadore Mirisch.

"What happened?" I asked Mirisch.

He smiled his rueful smile. "At the tennis court," he said, "someone made a backhand return with such force that the racquet flew out of his hand and struck me. It's not serious."

The girl from the bar appeared with two glasses of white wine over ice.

"Would you care for a drink?" Mirisch asked me.

"Mm, yes, thank you, that looks wonderful."

He held out his glass. "Take mine," he said, his long-lashed brown eyes smiling from their shadows, and ordered another for himself. He really was a lovely man.

Greenfield observed these proceedings with a benign expression to which his immediate resumption of a previous conversation gave the lie. "What you're saying," he said with deliberation to Mirisch, "is that there seems to be something operating . . . in the psyches of the world's population . . . which renders them either incapable of anticipating consequences . . . or immune to anything but their own personal needs."

"Their own needs," Mirisch said softly, "that's it exactly. That's why the world, in the past twenty years, has deteriorated from a state of—of mere chaos—to one of"—he lowered his head and shook it sadly back and forth—"certifiable dementia." He pointed with his good hand to something in the newspaper and went on, "What's the essential difference between the young apes who smash beer bottles all over the parking lot, leaving it strewn with glass, and the—the hyenas who dump toxic chemicals by the roadside where children play? They're both sick with the same disease, immediate personal need. The need for gratification, or the need for financial gain, at the cost of others. The need to survive at the expense of others. How else do you explain the technological and—and scientific geniuses who justify making the water we drink unsafe, the food we eat ultimately deadly, the air we breathe finally fatal?"

The girl came back with another glass and Mirisch took a quick sip of wine. "It's untenable to condemn technology and science out of hand," said Greenfield, who is capable of arguing either side of an argument and had, in the past and in my presence, expressed the same sentiments as Mirisch. "It's self-evident that both science and technology are responsible for life-sustaining inventions and discoveries without which we'd be in a sorry state."

"I wish I could believe," Mirisch said with ineffable sorrow, "they pursued those inventions and discoveries because they cared about humankind. But I believe"—he looked into his glass for a long moment—"I believe they do it for the scientific or technological challenge alone. And that makes a difference. That means they'll be as dedicated to a destructive challenge as they will to a constructive one. They simply . . . don't . . . care . . . about other people's lives."

"Who," Greenfield asked, "is 'they'? The entire scientific body? The entire output of MIT?"

"The overwhelming majority. The overpowering majority.

The invincible majority. Are careless of human lives. *That's why*"—he looked up and straight into Greenfield's face—"*that's* why the world is being destroyed."

"You," said Greenfield in mild surprise, "are a religious man."

Mirisch smiled faintly and shook his head, and I heard a familiar voice and turned to see Shura and Nadia coming through the French doors onto the terrace.

The Charnovs and Mirisch were introduced and Mirisch, who automatically reached out with his bandaged right hand, switched midway and shook Shura's hand with his left, made a courtly little bow as he took Nadia's, and then excused himself.

A great bank of dark clouds had gathered above the mountains on the horizon and the air was heavy as a wet towel.

"I have never seen it fail," Nadia said as we moved to a table in the screened-in dining room off the terrace. "All summer it has been like this. Beautiful all week, and then for the concerts, rain. People can no longer plan to sit on the lawn for a concert."

Greenfield assured her the weather report had made no mention of rain, but she said, "The weather bureau! They are the last to know! That's a nice man, that Mirisch. A violinist, I see."

"No," Greenfield said, "he's in publishing."

"Charlie, don't tell me no. The man is a violinist. Am I right, Shura?"

"I would say a violinist, yes," Shura agreed.

"You've met him before—"

"No, no, but he has the marks," Nadia said.

"You mean the characteristics?"

"I mean *marks*. On the ends of the fingers, on the left hand. What do you call it—? Calluses!"

"Even you, Charlie," Shura said, "and you don't play every day. All string players have calluses on the left hand, and you and I have five, because we use the thumb. But he had only four."

"I never shook hands with him," Greenfield said, "and if I had, he would have used his right—he hadn't hurt it then."

"And. the mark under the chin—" said Nadia, who had only to look up, since her black hair barely grazed Mirisch's shoulder.

"So. You think he's a violinist," Greenfield said, gazing absently at the menu.

"Think? There's no question," Nadia said with finality, and applied herself to choosing between chicken with mushrooms and shrimp with herbs.

Of course, I thought. Sensitive, sorrowful Mirisch. If he played anything, it would naturally be the violin. I wondered if he'd begun after his failure with the trumpet, or if the trumpet had merely been an interruption.

During dinner Greenfield steered the conversation to Sorrel, hoping, I supposed, to make some significant discovery, but neither Shura nor Nadia knew a great deal about him. He'd been around for a while in Europe, but hadn't made it to the top rank, and the talk was he was desperate to get there. He had an unorthodox beginning, as a horn player, then a composer. Most conductors came from the ranks of cellists, violinists, or pianists. He had a rigid personality— that was obvious. He "played by the book," adhering strictly to every instruction as written, yet he occasionally ignored a wrong note.

"He always complains he is overworked," Shura chuckled. "That comes from being a horn player. Horn players are always ready for a vacation. They play the slow movement of the Tchaikovsky Fifth and that's it for a month."

"When did Sorrel come up here?" Greenfield asked.

"Oh—I think—last Saturday or Sunday I saw him backstage talking to the librarian . . ."

"Mmm." Greenfield carefully impaled some pecan pie on the end of his fork. "Nadia, I'm going to ask you a favor."

"Whatever it is, it's done."

A woman who didn't shilly-shally. For no good reason I thought of the missing vodka bottle. She was certainly capable of it. But what possible motive would she have? Shura I discounted altogether. Even if the Guarnerius had been a cello.

"Would you call your son at Mass General," Greenfield said, "and ask him if he could give me the names of all the doctors who have offices on Boylston Street, and if possible the particular specialty of each one."

Nadia looked puzzled and Shura alarmed.

"You're sick, Charlie?"

"If I was," Greenfield said, "I'd hardly be playing the field in specialties. I'd more or less have the ailment pinpointed."

"Shura, for God's sake," Nadia said, and to Greenfield, "Of course I will call Richard. Why you want to know is your business. Maggie, you don't finish your dessert?"

How could I tell her that a day full of two angry old men, one newly bereaved widow, a temperature-humidity index of ninety-five, and a discussion of the imminent and total collapse of civilization, had somewhat impaired my appetite?

"I have to watch it," I said.

We went to the concert. It was a very different Tanglewood from the tranquil, unpeopled expanse of the rehearsals. Something like ten thousand people between the ages of six and eighty-six covered the lawn and filled the Music Shed. There were young mothers in peasant skirts and flat sandals, slinky thirty-year-olds in tight jeans and high heels, stout matrons with stiff dyed hair, willowy young men in pairs, unshaven young men in sweatshirts looking intense, comfortable middle-aged men eating ice cream, tourists looking around and smiling vacantly, ready to like everything. There were Indian saris, jogging shoes, plastic raincoats, gingham jumpers.

I saw the elderly trio from Wheatleigh, the two ladies in floor-length, dated dresses, clutching evening bags in their bony fingers, the old man in a French beret, white flannels and shoes, and a canary yellow jacket, leaning on a cane.

I saw the Felkers, looking tired; the tennis quartet, looking subdued; the new arrivals looking as though they were wondering if the place was on the market and how much they could get it for.

In the Shed there were a couple of movie stars sitting in select seats, the audience craning to look at them.

The musicians took their places. The lights dimmed. Sorrel walked to the podium. Applause. Music.

I might as well have been back home stacking the dishwasher for all the joy it gave me. I watched Sorrel and wondered what sinister connection Greenfield supposed there was between the poolside conversation about Boylston Street and the doctor's appointment card. I watched Shura and wondered if someone had put an explosive device in his cello. I watched Holchek and could see nothing but the empty space beside him. They were not playing the Ravel tonight, but those first four notes rang in my ears, blotting out Mozart.

I wanted to leave and go back with Greenfield to his balcony at Wheatleigh and thrash it out and find the solution in one moment of blinding revelation and save the BSO and forget it.

That, however, was not precisely what happened when we finally got back to Wheatleigh later that night. What happened was Jenny.

She was sitting alone in the Hall, facing the front doors, with Nefertiti hanging from her shoulder.

"My mother," she said, "is in the pool."

Guilt and relief washed over me in equal portions. Guilt, because I'd forgotten all about Eleanor being sick, and relief because she was obviously better.

"That's good," I said, "if she's swimming she must—"

"She's not swimming. She's crying. She's standing in the pool, naked, and crying. She won't tell me why. I was considering calling a psychiatrist but I don't know any around here. Do you?"

"No." I looked at Greenfield. He sighed and scratched a mosquito bite on his wrist.

"What's the matter with her?" he asked me.

"She's been—um—not feeling well since last night. Maybe we'd better go see what she's doing."

He looked at me as though I'd suggested a trip to the nearest swinging singles joint, said, "*You* go," and went off to the bar. I went out again, stopping Jenny from coming with me, and walked across the front portico and the garden. It was like walking through damp curtains. There'd been no rain—or rather, the rain had not come down. It was merely hanging up there in the sky, like the vague, undefined threat of bad news waiting.

I went through the wrought-iron gate and carefully down the slope. A red robe was thrown over a chaise, and Eleanor, a pale blur of nudity in the dark, was standing waist-deep in the pool, her arms stretched out on either side along the molded edging. She was not convulsed, she was not sobbing, she was quite immobile, but from the wide, staring daisy-eyes, the tears trickled steadily down her cheeks.

I crouched by the side of the pool.

"Eleanor," I said, "aesthetically speaking, the sight is not unattractive, but some idiot like Felker might come down here, or those three old people could decide to take a walk, and—"

"It doesn't matter." Her voice was normal, for Eleanor. Bemused, enervated.

"Listen, I have to talk to you—"

"I'm not out of my mind . . . I'm just tired . . ." She dipped a hand in the water. "I used to swim nude in the Stockbridge Bowl . . . that summer . . ."

"Yes, well, that was the Stockbridge Bowl. This is Wheatleigh, and somebody might get—" I somehow felt that getting her out of the pool and into a robe would break the spell, or whatever it was.

"My"—she choked on her tears—"my life is such a mess. I don't know why. . . . I can't . . . let go of him. After . . . what he . . ." The voice drifted into inaudibility, the wide eyes stared into the darkness.

Being neither a qualified psychologist nor an Indian used to squatting, I took the pragmatic approach. I got up and went to the chaise, picked up the robe and brought it back, holding it out for her. "Come on, let's sit down."

She didn't move for a moment, then she blinked her eyes, climbed out of the pool, got into the robe, tied the belt around it, walked with her usual languid gait to a chaise, and sank into it quite calmly, as though this were mid-afternoon and she'd taken the average dip in the pool. I sat down in the adjacent chair.

"Jenny says you haven't eaten since yesterday."

"I had some coffee . . ." She was remote, wandering in some past landscape. "Do you know the story of Scylla? Jenny told me. . . . She studied mythology . . ." She spoke dreamily, the sentences trailing off like the tails of kites. "Scylla was in love with a fisherman, and he was in love with her. . . . But Circe wanted the fisherman, and she was a jealous bitch. . . . She changed Scylla into a monster, and Scylla threw herself into the sea and became a rock . . . a rock, just standing there in the middle of the ocean, with the waves pounding at her forever, and she couldn't move . . . she never moved. . . ."

"You're scaring the hell out of Jenny, you know."

"It would be a lot worse if I told her . . . what it was all about . . ."

She lifted her arm listlessly and rested the back of her hand against her forehead.

"I'm not so sure," I said. "Nobody goes through life without once experiencing the pain of wanting someone they can't have. Even Jenny might know what it's like."

She made a small sound, like a dog that wants to be let in.

"If I could just . . . move. I can't move. . . ." She seemed to drift away, but after a moment, with the same lassitude, the voice devoid of passion or even inflection, she picked up the threnody. "I thought it would just go on the way it was. . . . I knew he'd never leave her, the bastard . . . he kept promising, but he'd promise anything. . . . I must be a masochist . . . well, everybody's one or the other. . . . I knew she'd hold on to him . . . I got used to it . . . she had him in public, I had him in private. . . . I didn't care . . . all he had to do was knock at the door . . . that was his style . . . walk in when he felt like it, walk out again and run home to Mama. I didn't care about that. It was the other one . . . I couldn't take the other one . . . just tore me apart . . ."

This was getting a little woolly for me. There was enough confusion in my mind about other aspects of Jan Sorrel without trying to follow the highways and byways of his love life.

"I don't know what you're talking about, Eleanor. I think we should go up to the house and get you something to eat." The classic poultice. Chicken soup. Eleanor didn't even hear me.

"I was nineteen," she rambled on in her tenuous voice, "and he was gorgeous. And I got pregnant. And he had his career to think of. He couldn't saddle himself with a wife and kid at his age. What a shit. He had to be free to realize his potential. And there was Leonard Springer, in medical school, and his parents were loaded. . . . All I had to do was say yes. Leonard would have signed away his life to get me into bed. He said marry Leonard, at least the baby will have a father. . . ." The voice trailed off again. "Bastard . . ."

I sat up. What was she saying. Jenny—?

"What choice did I have?" she continued dreamily. "My parents would have died. Pregnant with no husband? They would have had simultaneous strokes. . . . Besides, I always did whatever he wanted. I was afraid of him . . . I needed him. . . . He said once he was really established, I could divorce Leonard and we'd get married. I never stopped seeing him after I married Leonard. I sneaked around. Crummy motels. Then . . . the son of a bitch married *her*. He said he had to, for his career, she knew all the right people, but it wouldn't last, once he was up there he'd leave her. . . . Well, he never left her . . . she saw to that . . . a tough lady . . . she never let him out of her sight . . . and I didn't see him for years . . . years. . . . I became a rock, in the ocean . . . then I saw him again—here, where it all began—and nothing was different. He was still walking in when he felt like it, and walking out again . . . but this time it wasn't for me. . . ." She stared into the night, tears coursing down her cheeks.

My God, was it possible? Could any woman, however sexually enthralled, cling to this cockeyed conception of love for twenty years? In this independent age? And then I remembered that Eleanor didn't belong to this independent age. She was an anachronism, measuring her life in male devotions. But Jenny? How could that gamin in dark glasses, that black swan, be related to—?

"Are you telling me Jenny is Sorrel's daughter?"

She turned her head very, very slowly, her eyes wide, defenseless, and puzzled.

"Sorrel?" she murmured. "Why Sorrel?"

I stood up. I gaped at her. The truth rushed in on me from a dozen directions. Jenny's lovely gray eyes. The summer at Tanglewood, twenty years ago. A man who drops his used clothes on the floor for someone else to pick up. A man who borrows whatever he's short of—vodka, a car for a tennis date, a woman's body. Eleanor in the Music Shed staring at a spot to the left of the podium. Damaskin coming down from the second floor. Damaskin watching Jenny in the pool. . . . The tears were not for a lover lost, strayed, or stolen. The tears were for a lover dead.

Eleanor saw the realization hit me. She looked away and said in a near-whisper, "He was dying, and I was playing tennis with Dore Mirisch."

11

GREENFIELD WAS driving the Honda. I was in the passenger seat with my eyes closed because Greenfield had pronounced me incompetent. I hadn't had too much sleep the night before. I had mastered my state of shock sufficiently to get Eleanor back to her room with some toast and cheese and tea, which she probably didn't touch; I had reassured Jenny, who didn't even suspect—or did she?—that a murdered musician was her father; I had sat on the dark terrace with Greenfield and brandy, repeating the pathetic story, debating its implications; and finally I'd gone up to my room and fallen on the bed where I'd remained awake until four, or five, or sometime after that.

At seven thirty Greenfield had knocked on the door, there was a lot to be done this morning, would I be good enough to rouse myself and join him.

And now, an hour later, in the breathless, muggy morning, we were out and in hot pursuit of Cutter's. It was Greenfield's contention that his mind, which he needed for more important things, was being distracted by his physical discomfort. Seventeen times he had been attacked by those vicious insects, those aberrations of nature, and his neck, arms, and ankles were battlefields where small red bumps marked the final filling stations of dead but satisfied mosquitoes. He would find some Cutter's if he had to go all the way to Pittsfield to do so.

My eyes were burning from fatigue. I spoke without opening them.

"I have to go home," I said. "I can't cope with all these ramifications. We have hundreds of motives, but there's something wrong with all of them. Eleanor has been in sexual bondage to him ever since that first summer at Tanglewood—I don't know why it never occurred to me that Sorrel wasn't the only male around at that time. Anyway, the fact that he married Fran didn't put a stop to that, she had adjusted to that and anyway that was an old story. Therefore it doesn't make sense that she would kill him. On the other hand he'd found himself a new girlfriend, probably that youngster with the long blond hair, and she knew she'd lost him, and a woman scorned and all that, but she was used to being scorned, she virtually asked for it. *But* she's got an ex-husband who's a doctor. And according to her daughter she carried around half a drugstore wherever she went. And Fran has a medicine cabinet full of pills, but that doesn't mean any of them are lethal, and she probably knew about Eleanor, but it had been going on for so long, it was no longer a threat, she knew Eleanor couldn't win; however, she could have found out about that student with the blond hair and that could have scared her, and she was clearly not about to let anyone take Damaskin away from her. She could also fill the bill if you're thinking of a dog in the manger. Better dead than fled. Only how did she do it? She wasn't even around during the relevant hours. And Holchek was around, and I suppose an old man who's paranoid about being shoved from his hard-won perch by the younger musicians could be taunted or frightened into an irrational act, and he had the foxglove and besides he knows chemistry, but he was only near Damaskin at rehearsal and there were no signs that a hypodermic needle had passed between the two seats. And Sorrel had been to see a doctor, possibly in Boston, but probably eighty million people a year see doctors and that doesn't automatically equip them with the means for murder, and besides, what possible *reason* could he have? Damaskin didn't even beat him at *tennis*. And in any case, *nobody* could have poisoned Damaskin because Damaskin didn't *eat* anything or *drink* anything or get *injected* by anything that could have had poison in it. And even if they *could* have, it wouldn't have anything to do with the other incidents, because there's no reason in the world for Eleanor or Fran or Sorrel or Holchek to destroy the BSO! I've got to go home, Charlie."

"This place looks promising," Greenfield said, and pulled into the curb in front of a large, glossy Pittsfield drugstore.

The store had a cosmetics counter, a tobacco counter, an inordinate selection of paperbacks, and a dispensing counter behind which a single pharmacist had stopped filling a prescription in order to answer the phone, while a lethargic teenager and a restless businessman waited. Greenfield joined the waiting group while I browsed through the paperbacks. At a rough count there were several hundred Victoria Holts, seventeen spy stories in which a British agent and a Russian agent tracked each other through most of the chic European resorts and finally killed each other with mutual respect, twenty-one spy stories in which a CIA agent and a Russian agent pursued each other through various kinky boudoirs and an international incident was avoided. Thirty-odd disaster epics in which either the White House, the Taj Mahal, the entire Amtrak system, or a 747 carrying the Foreign Secretary to the Middle East with an eleventh-hour reprieve for the world was threatened by a) a tidal wave controlled by a space craft, b) a small package containing a deadly virus, or c) an underground organization of unknown allegiance with an arsenal the size of Ohio. And an uncountable number of murder mysteries involving only top-level personnel of the Petroleum Industry, the State Department, the Las Vegas Mafia, the Hollywood Mafia, the Police Mafia, the International Currency Regulations Bureau—or whatever. Apparently ordinary people no longer killed each other; murder, now, like the best tables in restaurants, was reserved for the VIPs.

I wandered over to the dispensing counter. The teenager had left and the pharmacist was handing the businessman a small plastic bottle with a prescription sticker on the front of it.

"There you go, Mr. Eiler. Two drops, three times a day. That should take care of it."

"Hope so. Hurts like the devil."

"I know. Nothing worse than an earache. Take care, now." He turned to Greenfield. "Yes, sir. What can I do for you?"

But Greenfield was staring at the receding business suit leaving the drugstore as though the man were a world-renowned figure in disguise.

"Sir?" the pharmacist repeated. "Can I help you?"

"Eardrops," Greenfield intoned, staring after the man.

"You have a prescription?"

Greenfield looked at him. "No. Do you have any Cutter's? Insect repellent."

He had, and he put it in a bag for Greenfield, and Greenfield paid for it, and you would have thought that having found his heart's desire after such a long and fruitless search he would have been gratified, but he was so preoccupied he almost left the store without it.

We got back into the Honda and Greenfield put the key in the ignition, gazed with steadfast scrutiny at a spot on the windshield, his chin pushing up into his lower lip, and finally said, "Eardrops."

I watched him through half-open eyes, wishing I could go to sleep and at the same time trying to keep awake because obviously some significant point had been made.

"The human head," he went on quietly, "contains four orifices, and we've been concentrating on one. I doubt an inhalant could have been the medium, given the medical findings. Besides, an inhalant certainly couldn't have been administered between eleven and five without Damaskin being aware of it. And he didn't smoke. That leaves—" He took the keys from the ignition, said, "Wait," and went back into the drugstore. What did he think I was going to do, sleepwalk back to Lenox? Did I look that dopey? I closed my eyes indignantly and dozed.

Eventually he reappeared, got behind the wheel, and looked at me, assessing my usefulness. "Are you conscious?"

"Yes." He continued his assessment. "Yes!"

"I'm going to require more of your faculties than the ability to blink your eyes."

"I'm okay."

He wasn't completely convinced, but he had few options. "Nadia," he said, "got in touch with her son last night and is expecting a call from him in half an hour. I'm going over there to speak with him when he calls. I tried to get hold of the medical examiner but his office hours don't begin for another twenty minutes, so I'm going to drop you off there to wait for him. . . . Mm. You seem to have recovered your faculties." His glance was more speculative than approving. "Give him this note and don't leave without the answers. I'll pick you up when I'm through at Nadia's."

He started the car and drove out of Pittsfield at his normal breakneck forty miles an hour. A few drops of rain sprinkled on the windshield.

Summer was evidently a slow season for the doctor, because I was the only one in the waiting room when he opened the door to his office. He looked the same as I remembered from that brief night-time glimpse, stocky and sixty and very much alive and well and living in highly enjoyable cynicism. He gave me a grin and waved me into the office. His desk, I noted, contrary to most doctors', was positioned like Greenfield's, up against the window, with the chair sitting on the inside rather than with its back to the window to create an intimidating space between doctor and patient. He, like Greenfield, felt no need to point up his superiority. I sat to one side of the desk and he swiveled to face me.

"So the curious Mr. Greenfield," he said, his eyes dancing, "gets curiouser and curiouser."

"We've run into some interesting possibilities," I said primly, "having to do with—um—with Mr. Damaskin, and Mr. Greenfield asked me to ask you"—where the hell was my sangfroid?—"if you'd be good enough to make two calls for him and get the answers to—to these questions." I handed him the slip of paper Greenfield had given me.

He grinned again before dropping his eyes to the page, then reached for the phone and dialed. "Frank? . . . Not bad. Yourself? Good . . . Frank, about that Damaskin business, you have the list there of the stuff we checked out at the house? Yah. You have a bottle of eardrops listed there? Thanks." He waited, leaning back in his chair, and fixed me with a wry gaze. "I don't usually give out this kind of information," he said, "but Mr. Greenfield, the detective"—a glint of amusement—"makes a damn good case for himself. Should have been a lawyer." He turned back to the phone. "That's what I thought. Thanks." He hung up. "No eardrops." He dialed again, asked for somebody called Orin, pulled a prescription pad closer while he waited, said, "Yah. No, no problem. The chemical in the Damaskin case, I need some information," and proceeded to ask questions and make notes. When he hung up again he tore the sheet from the pad and held it out to me. "There's your prescription, young lady."

Young lady? That was the best news I'd had all day. I thanked him for his trouble and he said it was a pleasure and opened the office door. A little gray-haired old lady in a print dress and a sweater was sitting on one of the chairs in the waiting room. Her face lit up at the sight of him.

"Hi, Phyllis," he said, "how's the old arthritis?"

"Not so good," she quavered, "not so good," and tottered happily into the office.

He winked at me and shut the door.

I thought seriously of moving permanently into the area, if only for the medical care. It would be worth pulling up stakes just to be able to turn my back on those monstrous waiting rooms in White Plains where you had to sit cheek by jowl with forty or fifty flu victims all at the communicable stage, while a battery of nurses behind a glass window kept answering telephones that rang incessantly and "The Doctor" was always an hour and a half behind schedule.

I went out into the damp hot air. There were splatters of

rain on the sidewalk, but nothing was coming down at the moment. The sky was reluctant to let loose; the inevitable downpour was still hanging up there. Talk about water torture.

I looked at the slip of paper he'd given me.

"The chemical"—he wasn't going to name it, not even for Greenfield—"the chemical is *not* a digitalis glycoside. It is obtainable as ampules in a drugstore or can be purchased commercially as a powder either in 1,000-mg or 5,000-mg packages. Is freely soluble in water, two grams of powder in 100 ml. Only about 5 percent will be absorbed in bloodstream, i.e., of 100 mg in 5 ml of water, only 5 mg will be absorbed, but 5 mg is enough to do it."

Poison in the ear, I thought. Because even in my condition, I had managed to figure out that was what Greenfield had in mind. I didn't quite see how it could be done. If nobody could make Damaskin *inhale* something while he was awake, I didn't see how he could be made to sit still while someone poured it in his ear.

I walked up and down the sidewalk trying to bring my faculties up to their usual glittering standard, until I saw the Honda coming down the street. There were three more drops of rain before I got in beside Greenfield and handed him the paper.

He read it, said, "Hm," then read it again and said, "Five milliliters. About a teaspoon. I don't see how." Then he studied the windshield for a while, finally said, "Possible . . . ," started the car, and drove toward West Stockbridge.

"I realize I'm only the messenger service," I said, "but it would be nice if you made an exception, in view of my years of faithful attendance, and gave me an inkling of what's going on."

"Sarcasm," he said, "is the last refuge of the insecure. Since you're anything but, the least you can do is leave it for those who need it. I spoke with Nadia's son. He found a half-dozen men with offices on Boylston Street. An orthopedic surgeon, a dermatologist, an ophthalmologist, a practitioner of cosmetic surgery, a psychiatrist, and a specialist in Ear, Nose and Throat. I called the ENT man. The nurse answered and said the doctor was in surgery. I gave the medical examiner's name—"

"You *what?*"

"Since anything I discover will be to his benefit, why not? I gave his name and said I had to know if the doctor had treated a patient by the name of Jan Sorrel last spring. Also one by the name of Noel Damaskin."

"Damaskin? I told you what Fran said. 'He doesn't know what it means to be sick. He's never been sick a day in his life.'"

"Illness"—he flipped the right-hand signal—"is something chronic. A sore throat or an infected ear"—he made the right turn—"is a mishap. As it happens, he *was* there. Both of them were. The girl—who will not go down in history as having contributed a great deal to the sum total of human knowledge—said she'd only been in the office a few weeks and didn't know all the patients, but I prevailed upon her. She finally found the files—no mean feat, according to her—and they'd both been there on the same day. She couldn't tell me why Damaskin had come, but apparently he had an infection, because there'd been a prescription issued." He paused to prepare the audience for applause. "For eardrops."

I stared at him and broke into a laugh.

"Frankly," he said, "not the reaction I expected."

I shook my head. "With your luck in guessing, you'd be a menace in Wall Street."

"Guessing after the fact hasn't produced a single millionaire. As for Sorrel"—he paused again—"he seems to be the victim of early otosclerosis."

"Oh," I said. "Mm. Is that—um—bad?"

"Progressive deafness."

My mouth opened and stayed that way.

"Not very pleasant for a conductor. An ambitious conductor."

"My God. No wonder he—Shura said he occasionally ignores wrong notes." I felt a surge of pity for the man whose life and livelihood depended upon hearing what he both interpreted and loved.

"I thought there was a lot of 'I don't hear' during rehearsals," he said, "'I don't hear the low-register flute,' 'Pianissimo does not mean absence of sound,' 'You're giving me a kitten, I want a tiger.'" He shook his head. "Beethoven was not only a giant, he was a saint."

"If word of this got around—" I began. The thought was chilling.

"You've just defined a motive. Damaskin may have passed him in the corridor outside the doctor's office. Or entering the building. He might sooner or later make the connection. Sorrel was buying time. He may also have been maddened by the injustice of his affliction. Needless to say, this is all theoretical. There's no evidence yet that he had any access to esoteric poisons."

"And even if he had, how did it get into Damaskin's eardrops? How did he even know Damaskin *had* eardrops?"

"Assumptions exist for a purpose. I'm assuming Damaskin mentioned his ear infection."

"But the infection was in the *spring*. He wouldn't still have it after all this time. Come to think of it, he wouldn't still be using eardrops."

"It could have recurred."

I fell silent. I looked out the window. I was definitely not cut out for this job. I spent most of my time feeling sorry for people who could turn out to be murderers. "Well," I said, "now I understand everything. Except why we're going to West Stockbridge instead of back where we belong."

"Because," Greenfield said, peering out the other window at a road sign, "all roads lead to Tanglewood, even this one, if I can find the right turn."

"You mean you traveled this whole route just to avoid making a U-turn on Main Street?" He refused to comment. "And what do we do at Tanglewood? Rehearsal's already started."

"I'm going to wait for intermission and talk to Batista and Tsuji. And you're going to visit Mrs. Connors."

"Who?"

"The cleaning woman. It seemed logical that Nadia would also use her occasionally, and she does. She had her address. We're still left with having to determine how, if at all, Sorrel got to those eardrops. He had invited Damaskin to play tennis—or Damaskin invited himself; whatever happened he knew Damaskin would be at Wheatleigh, and since he'd be swimming, would use the eardrops, but he couldn't—or didn't—depend on getting at the eardrops that way because he couldn't be certain he'd have an opportunity to get at them there, or even that Damaskin would carry them with him. He had to get into the house. He must have known Mrs. Damaskin was going up to the camp for the day, because the invitation—if there was one—would necessarily include her, or if there wasn't, Damaskin would have to explain why she couldn't come. He could have driven to Damaskin's house before morning rehearsal, waited up the street until Damaskin left for rehearsal, made some pretext to get into the house—"

"And been late for rehearsal," I said, pricking the balloon.

"Which," Greenfield said, with only a hint of triumph, "he was."

I thought about it. I remembered the rather extended tuning up and fiddling around while I waited under my tree on the lawn, the instruments' gradually falling silent as though Sorrel had arrived, but finally resuming, and the tuning still going on after that, and the practicing of a tricky passage here and there. Almost ten minutes.

"My God," I said quietly. And then, hopefully, "He just happened to have the poison lying around? And besides he only found out at the pool that Damaskin had seen him—"

"You're still not awake. According to your reconstruction, when Mrs. Sorrel said she'd never been to Boston, Sorrel said, 'I told you that before.' Presumably he had time to get his hands on something."

Greenfield pulled up at the Main Gate of Tanglewood, and got out of the car. I slid behind the wheel.

"You *are* capable of driving?" he asked. I nodded. He looked skeptical. "Pick me up on the porch," he said, and turned to walk away.

"Wait a minute! Why do you want to see Batista and Tsuji?" I asked.

He sighed and frowned at the man taking tickets by the entrance. "Because unfortunately," he said, "I can think of no reason for Sorrel to have threatened any other member of the orchestra."

He slouched off to the ticket window, this being Saturday and tickets necessary.

Other members of the orchestra. I'd almost forgotten about them.

I looked at the address and directions written on seagreen paper in Nadia's continental hand, and set off to "visit" Mrs. Connors.

It was a neat little house—and why not? Professional cleaning service 'round the clock—and Mrs. Connors had to get out of her large backyard swimming pool to answer the doorbell. Not only was I going to move into the area, I was going to enter domestic service.

I saw her from the driveway, floating on her back in the pool, but decided a formal approach was called for. I had to push the bell six times.

Her face sharpened at sight of me.

"Hi," I said, "I don't know if you remember—" Of course she remembered, why else did she look that way?

"I'm very busy just now," she said.

"It won't take a minute. I only want to ask—about the last day you were working at Mrs. Damaskin's. Did you—"

"I told the *police*, and I told *you*. There was no vodka bottle!"

Her small mouth clamped shut over a truculent chin. But the chin was trembling just a little. That vodka bottle was really bothering her. And it was beginning to intrigue me.

"I *know* it was there," I lied, "I saw it. Just the night before. A full bottle."

She looked past my left shoulder and said nothing.

"Nobody cares about the vodka," I went on quietly. "All they want to do is keep the wrong person from getting into serious trouble."

The green eyes flicked back to me, and then away.

"It was an accident," she said. "It could happen to anyone. I accidentally knocked it off the kitchen counter. If they want, they can take it out of my pay."

I breathed deeply. Not that I *really* thought Nadia had done it.

"So if that's all—"

"Wait." It was my first experience at stopping a door with my foot. "Who came to the house while you were there? Besides Mr. Damaskin?"

"Nobody."

"Are you *certain?*"

"*Nobody* came to the house who'd know *him*. A telephone man came in the morning. To fix the telephone."

"Was there something wrong with the phone?"

"I don't know. He said there'd been a complaint to the telephone company about static. He listened to the one in the kitchen and asked if there was an extension, and then he went to look at that, and after a while he left."

I tried to think if I'd seen an extension. Yes. In the bedroom. With the adjoining bathroom. Where Damaskin's eardrops . . .

"What time did he come?"

"I wasn't watching the clock. About a half-hour after I got there."

"Did he come in a telephone company truck?"

"I don't have time to check what kind of car people come in! I get paid by the hour and I don't waste the time." She tried to shut the door.

"What did he look like?"

"I don't know. Big. No hair. An older man. I can't talk

any more." She squeezed the door against my foot and I removed it and the door shut.

I walked slowly back to the car, feeling rotten.

It wasn't Sorrel. It certainly wasn't Sorrel.

Big. No hair. An older man. Holchek.

I found Greenfield on the porch of the Main House, looking inscrutable. The rehearsal was still going on; some large choral work. It must be Ozawa on the podium, preparing for a Sunday concert.

"Judging from your demeanor," he said, "you either didn't see the lady, or your car broke down."

"The car's all right," I said, "and I saw her." And I told him.

He stared out over the lawn and past Hawthorne's house to the mountains but he wasn't seeing anything. "I don't think it was Holchek."

"Why?"

"Well, for one thing, he wasn't late to rehearsal. And for another . . ." he sighed deeply, "Holchek's garden was vandalized last night."

"No!" I clapped my hand over my mouth. For some reason I was more shocked at this outrage than I had been at Damaskin's collapse. A vivid picture came to my mind of that glowing and lovingly nurtured creation. "Oh no!" I moaned. "How could anyone—"

"I'm afraid," Greenfield said, "that when God was designing man, he neglected to take your prejudices into account. He left room for all kinds. If Tennyson could actively dislike music, there must also be people who are immune to floral displays. Unless, of course,"—he started down the path to the gate—"he did it himself."

I went after him.

"Are you *crazy?*"

"To avert suspicion. To make it look like a threat against the orchestra and not the murder of a specific man. That's why those other incidents were perpetrated. Batista's deck, for instance, turns out to be five feet off the ground. Even if he'd been on it when it collapsed, he certainly wouldn't have been killed, but whoever did it knew there'd be no one there, and even pulled the deck to the ground so there was no chance of anyone's walking on it. Batista assumed it had fallen of its own weight. And Tsuji, when pressed, admitted that his car was never really in danger of turning over. It was a four-lane road and the car behind him raced ahead, then abruptly slowed and straddled the lanes, and Tsuji was forced half onto the verge to avoid denting his fender. There wasn't even a ditch. It was very carefully done to avoid damaging anyone. Just as the threatening letter and the ink on the oboe part hurt no one. None of these incidents resulted in bodily harm to anyone. That's what I found peculiar from the beginning."

"Well Holchek wouldn't—*couldn't* do that to his garden. It would kill him." In spite of the garden I felt better. It wasn't Holchek.

"Mm." Greenfield went to the passenger side of the Honda. "Well, there's still Avery, though I don't know how he could know about the eardrops. And of course, there are two others. I suppose women are stronger than they look. In any case, at least one of them has certainly demonstrated her ability to commandeer male help when necessary . . ."

My recovery was short-lived. I got glumly behind the wheel and drove back to Wheatleigh.

"If it was Mrs. Springer," Greenfield continued, looking pensive, "she had to have an accomplice. Not only because she couldn't pull down a window blind, let alone a deck, but because three of the incidents occurred before she got here."

"Then forget it," I said, pouncing on the reprieve, "because she had no reason to before she got here. She didn't know about the other girl until the night she went out to get peaches!"

Greenfield gave me a cold, inquiring look, indicating I had committed the cardinal sin of keeping something from him.

"The night Damaskin went to 'coach the chamber group,'" I explained wearily, "I think he went to meet the

Botticelli girl. I think Eleanor saw them. It doesn't matter. She didn't know about Botticelli until she got here."

"Botticelli," Greenfield muttered stonily, "and peaches. I hope you haven't found an equally impregnable alibi for Mrs. Damaskin, because if nothing else, she certainly knew about his eardrops."

At Wheatleigh on the velvet bulletin board under "Messages," there was a note with Greenfield's name on it. The medical examiner had called. Greenfield called him back and the message was short, simple, and a death blow. "If you're thinking what I think you are, eardrops remain in the ear canal and would never reach the bloodstream."

12

I WENT for a swim. The sky was gray and threatening, but the air was hot and sticky and I could think of no better way to overcome the accumulated tension and weariness short of going home. I'd suggested the latter to Greenfield, on the premise that he had established the lack of a threat to the orchestra, Shura included, but he claimed the threat to morale still existed and intimated my leaving at this point would be the equivalent of deserting Pearl White on the railroad tracks because you couldn't get the knots untied.

I'd expected the doctor's message to depress him beyond recovery, but except for a bleak lunch during which he succeeded in making the word martyrdom inadequate, he didn't seem to be deterred by this setback. I had the feeling he was secretly hoping this investigation would cover the length of his stay, and obviate his having to fall back on William Manchester.

I climbed out of the pool when those new arrivals, whose antics threatened to give enthusiasm a bad name, jumped playfully into it, splashing each other and laughing, until he struck out manfully with what I'm sure he thought of as a powerful stroke. She braced herself with the palms of her hands on the rim of the pool, lifted herself out backwards, and began a countdown, out loud, miming a stopwatch in one hand. It was hardly credible in a lady whose under-eye scars were still faintly visible. She was one of those people who get stuck with certain behavior patterns that worked for them when they were at sleepaway camp and never have the heart to abandon them thereafter.

By comparison, the Felkers, reclining wearily in their chaises, seemed acceptable company. He seemed finally to have abandoned his attempts to command my attention and I was grateful. I got into my robe, felt the need for some Kleenex, and reached into my pockets. In the right-hand pocket my fingers came into contact with Kleenex. In the left they collided with a small, knobby object. I held it in the palm of my hand and looked at it, and the moment returned: Nefertiti scampering to the edge of the pool, my foot landing on something rigid—I examined it and realized it was some kind of earplug, though not the usual kind. I tried to recall the sequence of events. Sorrel and Damaskin came out of the pool. They sat. No one else approached that end of the pool. Then Damaskin left, opening the gate. The cat streaked through, heading straight for the spot where they'd come out of the pool. I went after her, landing on the earplug—

I shivered, not because I was cold, wiped my nose with the Kleenex, and caught Felker's eye on me. He hadn't *completely* given up, he was just not vocal about it. I suddenly remembered his professional connection with drugstores. I approached him and he sat bolt upright in surprise. Ditto Mrs. Felker, in apprehension.

"Do you happen to know what this is?" I asked, holding out the earplug.

He took it between his fingers and immediately all his foolishness fell away and a respectable and knowledgeable businessman appeared.

"Molded acrylic earplug," he said. "You have to be specially fitted for this."

"Why would anyone go to the trouble? Are they better than the ordinary ones?"

"You wouldn't use these unless you had a problem. Then a doctor would prescribe it—get you fitted for one, so you wouldn't risk being exposed to bacteria, if you got water in your ear. But only if you had a problem."

"What kind of problem?"

"A perforated eardrum."

I almost screamed. I almost threw my arms around him. Only the certain knowledge that I would be struck by the lady in the next chair kept me from it. Instead I gave him my God-bless-you smile and ran like hell up the slope, through the gate, across the garden to where Greenfield was busy slouching in the chair on his balcony, and yelled up at him.

"Perforated eardrum! Perforated eardrum!"

For an instant he looked as though he'd like to disown any acquaintanceship with me, and then his eyebrows and one corner of his mouth went up, which meant he was laughing uproariously.

But immediately he frowned and muttered, "I should have thought of it." And then, not without satisfaction, "So should the doctor."

At that moment the heavens opened and the rain came down. I dashed to the portico and in through the door to the back stairway. Greenfield was at his open door, thinking.

"Those eardrops have to be somewhere. Get dressed and come down."

Half an hour later we were huddled under umbrellas in the Charnovs' driveway and Shura was unlocking the trunk of his car. There was nothing in it but a spare tire and a jack.

We went into the house, where Nadia was emerging from the bedroom in a claret-colored robe, fresh from the shower she'd been taking when we arrived.

"You used the car yesterday morning," Shura said to her. "Did you take something from the trunk?"

"Yes," she said, "I was going to take it to Fran, I put it on the floor in the bedroom while I made the bed, and I was just fixing the bedspread when the police came. I didn't want them to think I have a messy house, so I shoved it under the bed. Then I forgot."

But Shura was already in the bedroom, and came back carrying Damaskin's tennis bag.

Damaskin had run true to form and left his things for someone else to pick up. Shura deposited the bag on the old brass-bound trunk next to a bowl of fruit, Greenfield unzipped it, explored the interior, and produced a small plastic bottle of eardrops with a prescription sticker on the front.

We all looked at it solemnly for a moment. Poison. And then Shura said, nervously, "Put it down, Charlie. Don't touch it."

"Shura, for God's sake," Nadia said. "It can't jump out of the bottle."

"Fingerprints," Shura said.

Everybody was a detective.

Shura got some tissue and a small paper bag, and we wrapped it up. Nadia made hot tea in the samovar because it was raining. The fact that it was eighty degrees didn't affect her conviction that it was important to drink hot tea with lemon when it was raining. She served it in soda-fountain glasses with long spoons, and holders so they wouldn't be too hot to hold.

Greenfield pulled a folded sheet of yellow lined paper from his pocket and spread it out on the trunk. Across the center of the page in letters two inches high was written F♯ E D C♯. He turned it to face Shura and Nadia. "What does that mean to you?"

"F-sharp, E, D, C-sharp," Shura murmured. "That's the first four notes of the Ravel 'Rapsodie.'"

"Forget the sharps. What else? Anything else? Does it remind you of anything? Suggest anything? Do you connect it with any time, place, person, event?" They both stared down at it, sipping their tea.

"We play it," Shura said uncertainly, "many times at rehearsal. It repeats, you know, over and over."

"Was there any particular problem with it? Any discussion about it? Were there any arguments about it?"

Shura thought briefly, shook his head slowly, "No . . . no . . . nothing . . . some people thought it should be more pianissimo, but naturally you don't tell a conductor he's wrong when he wants more volume . . . no. Nothing."

"Nadia?"

Nadia shrugged. "Fa, mi, re, do," she said.

Greenfield froze in place, bending forward over the trunk, his hand cupped around the glass holder, his mournful eyes under their gray foliage fixed on Nadia's face.

"Fa . . . mi . . . re . . . do . . ." he intoned.

"Charlie," Shura said with concern, "I can see you're getting mixed up in this business. What are you doing? It's dangerous. You saw what happened. Even flowers are not safe. There is a maniac around—"

"I don't think so, Shura. I think Damaskin was the only one ever in jeopardy."

"You see, Shura?" Nadia said. "I was right." And then to Greenfield, "What did you find out? What do you know?"

"I know," he said patiently, "thanks to Maggie, that the bottle of vodka you gave the Damaskins was broken in a fit of housecleaning by Mrs. Connors, who didn't want to be found out and consequently disposed of the evidence."

"Oh, that. I could have told you that. A china figure of mine disappeared—I found the pieces in the garbage. Once an ashtray from Fouquet's, same thing. I told the police, ask Mrs. Connors. But she would never admit it. But what *else*?"

Greenfield shook his head. "It's all guesswork. That bottle of eardrops could be nothing but eardrops. I don't think so, but it could be. In any case, I'm going to take it down to the medical examiner." He stood up.

"That's right," Shura said, "let the police take care of it. It's their job. They have guns."

I caught Greenfield's eye with sudden alarm, but he stared me down and picked up the package containing the eardrops. Setting my glass on the trunk top, I thought of something.

"Is the Guarnerius still in here?" I asked.

"No, no," Shura said, "I took it back the next morning."

"You know they could have locked it up in their own house," I said. "They have a closet that locks."

Shura's brow creased. "Don't investigate," he pleaded.

We went out to the car armed with our borrowed Wheatleigh umbrella and drove to Stockbridge where we found the ME, in a yellow slicker, puttering about in the garage doing Saturday afternoon chores.

When he saw us, he said, "I just left another message. It occurred to me he might have had a perforated eardrum. We checked it out. He did."

Greenfield was magnanimous in victory. "That was a possibility," he said, and handed him the package. "Those are the eardrops. They were in his tennis bag. Under a bush at Wheatleigh. He forgot it." He wasn't about to involve the Charnovs.

The doctor looked at the package, then at Greenfield, then smiled skeptically. He didn't believe the part about the bush. "I'll let you know."

"Please do. And thanks for the assistance."

As Greenfield turned to go, the doctor switched the smile to me and said, "See you at the inquest."

On the way back to Wheatleigh Greenfield kept muttering "Fa . . . mi . . . re . . . do . . ." at intervals. The rain was no longer a heavy shower, it was a monsoon. The visibility through the windshield was virtually nil, the frantic wipers easily outstripped by the wild downpour.

"At times like these," I said, "a control room and a radar screen would not be a bad idea."

"Fa . . . mi . . . re . . . do . . ."

When we crashed, he'd still be saying it.

By virtue of the fact that the roads were all but deserted, we made it back to home base without either head-on or rear-end collision, and left the car in the parking space near the tower, and I tried to keep under the umbrella, which Greenfield held at random angles, being preoccupied with fa-mi-re-do, as we covered the distance to the portico. The result was that I was drenched, and when we got to his room he looked at me, rain trickling down my cheeks from my dripping hair, and said, "Like Niobe, all tears."

"Charming," I said. "May I borrow a towel?"

He gestured to the bathroom and went to stand in front of

the shirt-board with the letters F, E, D, C on it. The lovely room, as usual, looked as though it had been visited by a passing tornado. Each day the chambermaids restored it to its former gracious splendor, each day Greenfield turned it into Sam Spade's office. When I came out of the bathroom, rubbing vigorously at my hair, he was rummaging among the papers on the bed. He uncovered the crossword puzzle Damaskin had been doing at the pool, put it aside, picked up the sheet on which he had copied the scribbles and doodles Damaskin had made on the inside of his music folder, picked up the puzzle again.

"The answer," he mumbled, staring at the two pieces of paper, "has got to be somewhere in this man's character. Which, to put it as nicely as possible, was deplorable. Nevertheless—his way of life, his habits, his beliefs, his indulgences . . . his preoccupations . . ."

"What's it from," I asked, "'like Niobe, all tears'?"

"I thought you knew your Shakespeare. It's *Hamlet*."

"Poor Mr. Holchek."

He looked up. "Holchek?"

"His garden. He had all the flowers that Shakespeare mentioned in his plays—primrose, cowslip, violets, buttercup . . ."

He ignored me and returned to the two papers. "The man was intrigued by word games. Puzzles, anagrams, palindromes—"

"Do you realize how often Shakespeare has entered our conversation in the last few days?"

He turned to look at the shirt-board. "Backwards?" he mused, "do . . . re . . . mi . . . fa . . . ?"

"It's remarkable. I usually don't mention Shakespeare for months on end."

Greenfield very deliberately put the two sheets of paper on the lingerie chest, placed both hands flatly on its top, allowed his chin to sink to his chest, and spoke to the floor, with forbearance above and beyond any known to history, including Job's. "I may or may not be on the verge of discovering what this message of Damaskin's is all about, and it may or may not be important, in fact it may or may not be a message. Nevertheless, it's one of the few things we have to go on, and in recognition of my efforts to explore its possibilities, it would be obliging of you not to interrupt with irrelevant references to Hamlet, to Holchek, to flowers, or to Shakespeare's ubiquity."

"Sorry," I said. And then, in a stubborn attempt to save face, "Maybe it's not irrelevant. Since we find Shakespeare everywhere else, maybe we'll find it in do-re-mi."

There was a long pause while Greenfield studied the floor. Then he picked up the sheet of scribbles and peered at it. "Do, re, mi," he said. "No fa. It's possible. The circle goes through the fa. I thought his pen had slipped—he was hardly in control at the time. . . . Was the fa deliberately left out?"

It was beginning to sound like Jabberwocky. Unregenerate, I pursued my own thoughts. "Didn't Niobe cry herself to death and turn into a stone, and didn't tears keep coming out of the stone?" He didn't answer. "That would have been a more appropriate simile for Eleanor, than Scylla. The tears certainly kept coming out of her."

He looked up from the floor and I thought I was in for another blast, but he said, very quietly, "What was it she said to you? The last thing she said to you, at the pool."

"Eleanor?"

He nodded, closing his eyes to blot out the sight of the person he might yet have to throttle. I tried to remember.

"Something about playing tennis with Mirisch. 'He was dying and I was playing tennis with Mirisch.'"

"There was a first name. Try again."

"'. . . and I was playing tennis with . . . Dore Mirisch.' Short for Isadore. As in Dore Schary."

"Dore . . . Mirisch." He took out his trusty Parker 51 and wrote on the shirt-board, "Do, re, mi, fa." Then he crossed out the fa. Then he drew a line between re and mi.

We stood looking at the result for what seemed like minutes. My lack of sleep, I thought, must finally be catching up with me. I felt weak and dizzy. I thought of Mrs. Connors. *"Big. No hair. An older man."*

"That's ridiculous," I said faintly. "There's absolutely no connection—"

He walked to the door and out into the corridor, leaving the door open. I started after him, then stopped, located his room key on the bamboo table, went out and shut the door. He continued down the corridor and across the Hall to the bar and I followed. There were people in the Hall. Two-thirds of the elderly trio (the gentleman was missing, off for an afternoon snooze while the hardier sex carried on, each in an armchair doing needlepoint) and the tennis quartet, looking sulky, deprived by the weather of their prime source of communication. No Eleanor. No Jenny. . . . No Do, re, Mirisch. There was no one in the bar but Greenfield, scanning the glassed-in bookshelves. Baroque chamber music issued softly from the stereo.

I sat on a barstool next to the long, partly open window, put my arms on the counter and my head on my arms, and breathed the warm, wet air, trying to calm myself. Greenfield was playing games, I told myself. It was make-work, because he had to have some problem to keep his mental muscles happy. There was nothing more to it. There couldn't be. Mirisch had been nowhere near Damaskin. As far as we knew he didn't even know him.

Greenfield opened a bookcase and withdrew a large volume. I had no idea what he was doing and I didn't want to know. He flipped pages seven or eight times, then stopped. After a moment he came to the bar, put the book on the counter, and read aloud.

"'. . . upon my secure hour thy uncle stole, with juice of cursed hebanon in a vial, and in the porches of my ears did pour the leprous distilment; whose effect holds such an enmity with blood of man that swift as quicksilver it courses through the natural gates and alleys of the body—thus was I, sleeping, by a brother's hand, of life, of crown, of queen, at once dispatch'd.'"

The ghost of Hamlet's father came back to point a finger at the murderer. Do, re, mi.

Greenfield shut the book and put it back on the shelf.

I remembered Mirisch in the dining room that first night, reading. *"It was sitting on the night table when I was packing and I dropped it in my suitcase."*

"Mirisch couldn't be Damaskin's brother," I mumbled, pointlessly. "He's got a different name."

"We don't really know anything about him," Greenfield said, "except that he's an angry man."

"Angry? Mirisch? He's the sweetest, most gentle—!"

Greenfield pointed toward the terrace. "You *were* sitting at that table yesterday? You *did* hear the man talkng about the armies of the amoral and the self-serving? What did you think that was—cocktail chit-chat? The world is setting fire to his house and he's powerless to stop it. Of *course* he's angry."

"But there you are!" I said eagerly. "He was shocked by people throwing toxic chemicals around! How could he possibly *poison* anyone?"

"The same way angry citizens defend themselves against gun-carrying criminals by buying guns of their own."

"But Damaskin was no threat to him—"

"We don't know what Damaskin was to him."

I shook my head. "No. Not Mirisch. I don't believe it. He'd be the last person in the world to have a bumper sticker demanding the right to bear arms. Anyway, how would he get his hands on that kind of poison? He's not a doctor, he's not a chemist—"

"We don't know what his connections are."

"He works for a publisher. They don't deal in drugs."

Greenfield was silent. The chamber music played on. Finally he got up and went to the telephone in the corridor. Irene came in and began to fuss with things behind the bar.

"Get you something?"

I hesitated. "Yes, thanks, some sherry."

She poured it and set it on the counter. I took a sip. Each time there was a diminuendo in the music I heard the drone of Greenfield's voice at the telephone. I looked through the long windows at the soaking-wet terrace. The monsoon was over, leaving behind a dreary drizzle.

I'd finished the whole glass of sherry when the tennis quartet came in and ordered drinks, and drowned out the chamber music with their chatter. I went out to the corridor. Greenfield was hanging up the receiver.

"I have an acquaintance in New York," he said, "in the publishing field. He deals in medical texts." He wandered into the Hall and up to the front doors and stood looking out at the curtain of drizzle descending from the porte cochere. The two old ladies were still pushing their needles down and pulling them up, at the far end of the Hall. I came up beside him.

"I asked," he went on, "if he knew of any publisher in Boston who had a medical textbook department. He not only knew one, he'd worked for them. I asked what the job consisted of. He says he began as a field representative, and for five years he made the rounds of the faculties of various medical schools looking for medical manuscripts and promoting texts for various courses. In the process he claims to have accumulated a fund of knowledge that surpasses that of any individual physician. Take that with a grain of salt. However, he is now Medical Sales and Promotion Manager and has had extensive dealings with pharmacologists and biochemists, and yes, he could conceivably be in a position to get his hands on an esoteric drug." Greenfield paused and pushed some damp gray strands of hair off his forehead. "I asked if he'd ever come across Mirisch. He said, 'Oh yes, he's in the same racket.'"

The feeling that the ground was shifting under my feet was no longer a solitary disturbance, it now had a vague nausea to keep it company. Greenfield turned away from the doors and went toward the corridor to his room. I looked at my watch. It was almost seven thirty. What year, I wasn't sure.

"I have to lie down," I said to his back, and moved uncertainly toward the staircase. I made it as far as the Tiffany windows when a voice stopped me. The beard.

"Phone call," he said, "for either you or Mr. Greenfield."

"Oh." I looked down the flight of stairs and wondered if I'd ever get this far again once I'd gone down.

"You can take it in the office."

"Thank you." It could be anyone. It could be Elliot. I'd better go.

It was Nadia.

"Maggie? For God's sake don't tell Shura I told you. I am over with Fran. The Guarnerius is gone."

I whimpered.

"She says the sister took her and the boy to the camp to get his bicycle and when they came back the place was upside down and the Guarnerius was gone. Tell Charlie I said if he has ideas where it could be, fine, but he must not put himself in danger. You also."

As I lowered the receiver, Greenfield came into the office.

"I seem to have locked myself out of my room."

I reached into my pocket and took out the key. "Sorry," I whispered.

He looked at me. "Maggie, I once saw a woman dragged from the English Channel, which she had been trying unsuccessfully to swim, and by comparison with you she looked like a healthy Swede after a sauna."

"Um . . . We just had a phone call." I led him out of the office and into the Hall and gave him Nadia's news, and he was still standing there absorbing it and examining the carpet when Eleanor Springer came drifting down the staircase.

"You haven't seen Jenny . . . have you?" she asked with profound lassitude. "She said, half an hour ago, she'd be right back. She went to look at the tower with Dore Mirisch."

13

ADRENALINE IS a truly remarkable thing. It can take you from comatose to Marathon Runner before your wits have anything to say about it. We didn't actually run to the tower, but it was no early evening stroll, either.

I was certain that Mirisch, if he was sane, would never harm Jenny, as Jenny. But Jenny as Damaskin's daughter? Could he possibly know about that?

Greenfield had appropriated a large flashlight from the office and told me not to come, and stalked off, and I had stalked along with him, and he had glowered, but said no more. As we entered the inky, dusty darkness, he switched on the flashlight and the beam picked out a small white ellipsoid shape on the encrusted floor—a bird's egg. He swung the light in an arc, and there were glimpses of a broken lamp, a vase, the icebox. No one there. The light came to rest on the wooden stairs against the outer wall going up into sooty blackness. He shone the light down at the floor in front of us and we moved to the narrow flight of stairs. It was decrepit; splintered and shaky, with a railing that felt loose, as though one good shove would send it toppling. He went up slowly, and when he sensed me following, flashed the light on his own face and shook his head. He continued up slowly, and then, as he put his weight on one of the treads, it cracked. I stifled a cry and felt my way up to him.

I heard him sigh in exasperation and murmur, "Stay . . . down . . . there." He stopped climbing. We stood still, on those treacherous stairs, in the dark, in the total silence, and suddenly there was a horrible flapping of wings.

I gasped. I almost fell down the stairs. I clutched the shaky railing so fiercely that some of the rotten wood splintered off. I was in a murky silo fifteen feet above a floor thick with ancient bird droppings, on a stairway that was crumbling by inches, and there was something large flying around within yards. My pulse raced, breathing was an effort, I was afraid to move even a finger.

Greenfield's voice above me said, "Jenny," into the darkness, and after a pause, with more emphasis, "*Jenny.*"

There was a slight scrape on the floor above, and then Jenny's voice, quiet and calm, but with an edge to it.

"Don't come up here."

That, of course, was all Greenfield needed. He took another step upward and then stopped. The light shone on a hole in the stairway. Two treads were missing. In order to reach the one above he would have to straddle the hole, putting all his weight on the feeble railing—and even if the railing held, was that tread on the far side of the hole a sound one? He'd be landing on it with virtually no support.

"Charlie!" I said furiously, "No!"

The light swung as he straddled the hole and landed.

Leaving me suspended between one death trap and another. Terrified of either ascent or descent.

"Come on," he said, "you can't stay there." He held out a hand, but I wouldn't take it. If I fell, he'd come with me. My fingers bit into the railing. I moved, and felt his hand grab my arm. I was standing above the hole, shaking.

Jenny spoke again from out of the darkness. "Please. Don't come up. I don't want you to come up."

"Mirisch?" Greenfield said. No reply. Greenfield assumed his blandest, most casual manner. "Mirisch, why did you take the girl up there? This place is booby-trapped."

Jenny said, "He didn't *take* me up here. I saw him from my room, going in here, and I decided I'd like to see it."

I couldn't believe that someone like Jenny would have

stayed at Wheatleigh on and off for years without exploring the tower.

"That was half an hour ago," Greenfield said. "Your mother was worried."

"I told her where I was going."

"That was half an hour ago," Greenfield repeated.

Silence.

"We've been talking," Jenny said.

I could all but see Greenfield's chin pushing up into his lower lip.

"Mirisch," he said, "I have to talk with you. I can't do that with Jenny around. Send her down."

After a long silence, Mirisch's voice came down, as gentle and reasonable, and sad as ever.

"She's the only protection I have. I only need her for a little while longer."

"It would be an act of stupidity to harm her."

"Oh . . . I would never harm her. She's with me voluntarily."

"Then she doesn't protect you."

"Well, yes, she will."

"Jenny!" I said hoarsely, "come on down, you're being silly."

"No," she said, "I was out walking in the rain, and I was on the terrace outside the bar when you were reading *Hamlet,* so I know what's going on, and I don't want Mr. Mirisch turned over to the police. I told him what you were saying and he told me the whole story."

I looked at Greenfield, but it was too dim to see much.

"If it's the kind of story he can tell you," Greenfield finally said, "I see no obstacle to his doing the same for us."

"I intend to tell you," Mirisch said. "There'd be no point in doing away with Damaskin unless people knew why. It's important that people should know why."

A pause. I heard the flapping of wings again, but farther away.

Then Mirisch spoke again, calmly and quietly. "But right now, I have to leave. There's one more thing I have to do. I don't know if you intend trying to stop me, but just to be on the safe side, would you and Mrs. Rome please let me go by. Jenny will come down first. She's going to go past you, to the stair just below the two missing treads. She's going to let me by and then she'll stand there without holding onto the rail. If you try to bridge that gap to come after me, you'll surely send her down the stairs. If you try to detain her as she passes you, she'll struggle and that could be disastrous for everyone."

There were muted, scuffling sounds from above, and then Jenny's footsteps approaching. Greenfield pulled me back to the wall and Jenny moved past us, a lighted flashlight in her hand. The light picked out the black void at her feet. It was infinitely worse going down, reaching out for that dim lower stair that seemed much too far away to reach with one leg. Miss by an inch and you would plunge through the hole, hanging by one arm from the splintering rail. I held my breath while she stretched one long leg down across the gap, and then she was standing below it, both feet planted on the far tread, shining the light up for Mirisch.

He came quietly, not looking at us, a pale yellow shirt and tan trousers emerging from the gloom, and made the descent without hesitation, as though it hardly mattered whether or not he missed the step and fell through the dark nothingness to the crusted floor of the tower.

He didn't miss. He squeezed past Jenny, who stood aside for him, and the stairs creaked as he continued down, and eventually we heard his steps crossing the floor below. Then the stairs creaked again and Jenny disappeared into the gloom.

Greenfield pointed the light at the hole. "Go," he said.

I'd never in my life been so reluctant to make a move. I clenched my teeth, thought of my family, wished I were home, and took the enormous, intolerable step. I reached the far tread. I breathed. Greenfield continued to shine the light down the stairway.

"Can you see enough to get down?" he asked.

"I'll wait for you."

I heard a car start up in the parking space outside.

"I'm going up," Greenfield said. "Go after Mirisch."

"What are you—?"

"Maggie. Go."

I felt my way down the dim, shaky stairs, saw a grayish streak of light at the open door, and made for it. A dark blue Ford went by with Mirisch at the wheel as I stepped out into fresh air. The rain had stopped. I ran to the Honda like a programmed robot following orders. Defense mechanisms work in mysterious ways.

I was close enough behind Mirisch to see his license plate turn to the right on West Hawthorne, and I followed him up the road towards Tanglewood. At the corner of West Hawthorne and just plain Hawthorne, several cars coming from my right intervened, but I could still see him. The concert audience was gathering. There was a line of cars up ahead, some of them shearing off into the driveway to the parking lot for the VIPs, the rest waiting for a chance to maneuver into the lot opposite the Lion's Gate. Young patrolmen in blue caps and blue short-sleeved shirts were directing traffic—the usual concert detail. But tonight they were augmented by a sprinkling of regular police and even County Sheriffs looking more like movie extras in their wide-brimmed light gray hats. I wondered briefly whether the increased security was the result of Damaskin's suspicious death, and if it had been there, unobtrusively, ever since, and escaped my distracted attention. It occurred to me that many a serious consultation must have taken place between the police and the Tanglewood administrators regarding security. What were they looking for now? Could they possibly have been led to Mirisch, without Nadia to look at four notes and translate them in vocal terms? Without Greenfield's knowledge of Damaskin's penchant for anagrams and palindromes? Was there another trail leading to Mirisch?

The dark blue Ford was half-hidden in the welter of cars converging on the huge parking lot, but I could see enough of it to realize Mirisch was not trying to get through it, but merely following it into the lot—into the lion's den—cops everywhere—what was going on in his mind? He was in the lot now. Soon he'd be on foot, and I was still trapped in a machine among crawling machines.

I was too far behind him. With the traffic being siphoned alternately from eastbound and westbound lanes and the maddening snail's pace of the parking, he could be in the next county by the time I got out of the car. I'd virtually lost him.

I regarded the bottleneck at the entrance to the lot, and the resultant empty traffic lane on my left. If I could manage a U-turn, I could probably get back to Wheatleigh, pick up Greenfield—provided he'd gotten out of the tower without breaking his neck—drive back to within a reasonable distance of Tanglewood, so that at least one of us could get out of the damn car and go looking for Mirisch, and all in less time than it would take to sit through this creeping procedure.

Debating, I caught sight of Mirisch heading for the Lion's Gate, a large red plaid blanket over his arm.

I signaled, pulled out of the line, wrenching the wheel as far to the left as possible, backed, inched, maneuvered, and roared off down the road to Wheatleigh.

Just past the tennis court I braked. Greenfield was loping across the lawn toward me, Jenny beside him, arguing. I leaned out the window.

"Why?" Jenny was demanding. "*Why* are you going after him?"

It was a good question, and one I myself would have asked if I'd had the time. Greenfield ignored her and said to me, "Well?"

"I lost him. He's somewhere on the Tanglewood grounds."

He opened the passenger door and Jenny said, "I'm coming."

"You're not," Greenfield said shortly, and climbed in.

"Wait." I'd had an intelligent thought, my first in quite a while. "Do you drive?" I asked Jenny.

"Of course, what do you think?"

"Get in," I said, as Greenfield looked at me to determine if I was truly sane.

Jenny squeezed in beside Greenfield, who clenched his jaw at the indignity, and I turned the car around and was heading back down the drive when another car came to meet me from the bottom of the drive: a car bearing two men in police uniforms.

They stopped in the middle of the road, barring my exit, and Jenny immediately said, "Don't say anything!" One of them got out and walked at a leisurely pace to my window. He looked over the occupants of the front seat and said to Greenfield, "Mr. Mirisch?"

"Greenfield," Greenfield corrected. "What's the trouble?"

"We're investigating a theft."

A *theft*, for God's sake! And then I remembered the Guarnerius.

"You know," the officer went on, "if there's an Isadore Mirisch staying here?"

"Yes, there is," Greenfield said. "Has he had something stolen?"

"Nope. Lady in Lenox reported a valuable violin missing. A neighbor of hers told us he saw a strange man come out of the house this afternoon when there was no one home, carrying a case. Man got into a dark blue Ford. The neighbor thought it looked suspicious and he was on his way to town anyway, so he followed the Ford, got his Massachusetts license number, saw him turn in here, reported it to us. We checked out the license and we're looking for an Isadore Mirisch. You say your name's Greenleaf?"

"Green*field*." Greenfield pulled out his wallet and displayed his driver's license.

"You know if Mr. Mirisch is up at the house, Mr. Greenfield?"

"I think he checked out," Jenny said. "He said something about going away. He has a cabin on an island off the coast of Maine. With a boat, equipped with provisions. I think he was planning to sail down to South Amer—mph!"

I winced at the thought of Greenfield's heavy shoe on her sandaled foot.

"I have no idea where he could be," Greenfield said, retrieving his license. "Is it all right if we go on our way? We don't want to miss the concert."

The officer stood aside, signaled to his colleague, who steered the police car to his right so that we could pass, and I drove out to West Hawthorne.

"Good old Avery," I said, "the conscientious citizen."

"You didn't have to tell him Mr. Mirisch was staying there!" Jenny protested.

"No?" Greenfield said. "You don't think they were going to go up to the house to check, no matter what I said?"

"If you'd come with me," I said, "we'd never have run into them. And I wouldn't have lost Mirisch. What were you *doing* up there in the tower?"

"Mirisch went up there for a reason," he said. "I was looking for the reason."

"And?"

"And I found it. Good God," he said, staring at the stream of cars up ahead, "we'll be here until September."

"Not this time." I pulled up the emergency brake. "Jenny, will you park the car for me?"

"Not," she said, "if it means helping you track down Mr. Mirisch."

"It won't matter. If you won't do it, one of us can still go after him."

"How do you know," Greenfield said, leaning across her and opening the door, "we're not going to warn him about the long arm of the law waiting back there? Let me out, please."

Jenny and I got out through opposite doors at the same moment and I hurried around the front of the car and down the verge to the Lion's Gate, leaving them to sort it out between them, wondering what was driving me after Mirisch, was it sheer momentum, was it a need to finish something I'd begun, was I so deeply dedicated to law enforcement, what *was* it? And it came to me. It was because I couldn't understand it. I couldn't reconcile a man like Mirisch with murder. I couldn't figure out *why*.

At the gate I turned to look back and saw Greenfield threading his way toward me through the groups of neatly dressed people heading for the grounds. I went to the ticket booth and bought tickets, and when Greenfield arrived, handed them to the old gentleman who was there for the purpose, and we walked in, two of the most bedraggled concertgoers ever to grace these grounds.

We stood still for a moment, looking with frustration at the vast expanse of lawn and the thousands of people moving around on it. Though the rain had stopped and there were patches of lighter gray in the sky, the lawn was sopping wet and the outdoor audience was setting up folding chairs, or spreading tarpaulins or slickers or plastic tablecloths on the grass to sit on.

Suddenly I caught sight of a distant red plaid blanket over someone's arm disappearing behind the far end of the Main House.

"There!" I pointed toward the back of the Main House and set out across the wet grass.

"You *saw* him?" Greenfield asked skeptically, striding beside me.

"No, but the blanket. He was carrying a blanket. Red."

"There are probably several dozen of those on the grounds."

"Well, we have to start somewhere."

But there was no red blanket in sight when we rounded the corner of the house. And it didn't matter. Because Mirisch himself, not twenty yards in front of us, was crossing our line of vision from the house to the formal garden that runs along the westernmost border of the grounds. And he was carrying something pale yellow and something tan on his arm. And he was wearing a white shirt, white pants and a black tie.

I stopped short and looked in utter bewilderment at Greenfield. "Changed his *clothes?*"

Greenfield nodded, not in reply, but because he understood something. He didn't, however, enlighten me, but followed Mirisch to the garden entrance through which he had disappeared, and I hurried after.

The garden—Koussevitzky's "fummil garden"—was a maze of hedges and paths opening here and there into small cloistered greens dotted with stone benches and artificial ponds. The hedges were high—turn a corner and you would be invisible to anyone on the path you'd just left—and when we looked to right and left, there was no sign of Mirisch. With a gesture, Greenfield suggested we divide the terrain, and went off to the left.

I turned right, went through a narrow opening in a hedge, around a pond and down stone steps to a path, which made a long U and returned me to the far side of the pond and a trellised grape arbor. The place was deserted, which wasn't surprising considering the soaking it had taken. I sprinted down the hundred and fifty feet of arbor to an area of wild grass ending in trees, saw nothing, ran back to the path, which now led in the same direction and parallel to the one Greenfield had taken, and emerged at the end of the garden, which bordered the road, where a rectangle of lawn led to a wide, curved stone seat.

Greenfield stood on the grass looking toward the shadowy corner beyond the stone seat where the tall garden hedge met the tall road hedge in an impenetrable mass of shrubbery. I followed his glance and saw the movement of something white, close to the ground.

Then Mirisch stood up, and he was holding under his arm a violin case shrouded in a drycleaner's transparent plastic bag.

He saw us and paused, and then went calmly to the stone seat, put down the case and the clothes he was carrying, removed the plastic, opened the case and took out the violin and bow, placed the folded clothes in the case, and slipped the case into the plastic.

He turned then, to face Greenfield across the grassy rectangle.

"I had to hide it here earlier," he said apologetically. "I

had a blanket for the clothes, but I didn't want to risk trying to get the case past the—past the police."

"They're looking for it now," Greenfield said, and ambled over to the stone seat and sat down. I crossed the grass and joined them.

"Mirisch," Greenfield said, "I have to know."

"Soon."

Greenfield shook his head. "The police can count. There will be plenty of lapsed time to account for as it is." He reached into his pocket, produced a crumpled handkerchief, unfolded it and displayed for our benefit a small, unmarked vial, and what looked like an eyedropper.

"I found these inside a length of pipe in the tower. They had no dust on them and were obviously put there recently. My guess is you put them there the night of the postmortem. I thought I saw a flicker of light in the tower that night. The vial is empty now, but it wouldn't shock me to learn that it had contained the poison you substituted for the eardrops in Damaskin's pharmacy bottle. The dropper, I wouldn't be surprised, is also Damaskin's. You would have had to substitute one of your own, doctored, so that a larger volume of fluid would be released when the bulb was pressed." He folded the handkerchief over the objects and put them back in his pocket. "Evidence," he said quietly, "can't be concealed for an unreasonable length of time without exacting a penalty. If you need time, I have to know why."

Mirisch looked at his watch, passed a hand over his face, and sat down.

"I was a violinist," he began softly. "Noel Damaskin was my pupil. When he was just a boy. He was my pupil for four years. He was gifted. I didn't charge for the lessons, he came from working-class parents who couldn't afford it; two simple people, who loved music, and who somehow managed to produce two gifted children. The other was a girl. She was seven years older than Noel, and she was a remarkable pianist, and a lovely . . . lovely woman. She adored Noel. So did his parents. He was very spoiled. But, as I say, gifted. And naturally he went on to other teachers. Better teachers. When Noel was twenty, and his sister twenty-seven, she and I were married. Noel was away—at Tanglewood—that summer. Leona and I were very—it was a very happy marriage. I loved her very deeply. I'd never been that happy in all my life . . ." He cleared his throat and went on. "Noel was doing well. Trips to Europe. He would spend a year or two in some symphony orchestra—St. Louis, Los Angeles—and then go off to Europe and see the sights. He looked prosperous, he dressed well, sent his parents lavish gifts, had managed to get himself on the board of an Arts Council out west . . .

"Then one day he showed up at our home and told us he was in desperate trouble. He had been 'borrowing' large sums of money from the treasury of the Arts Council of which he was Treasurer—he had meant to replace it before it became obvious, but somehow . . . and now he was in danger of being found out. He needed fifty thousand dollars immediately, and he had no one else to turn to. Credit at a bank was not possible, he had already defaulted on too many loans.

"We didn't have that kind of money. Our only material possession of any great value was something I . . . something I cherished almost as much as my wife. Something of great beauty. Incomparable beauty. A Guarnerius, del Gesù . . ." He looked down at the instrument in his lap and stroked it with a finger, reverently. "I'd sacrificed many other things for it. The home I would have liked to have. Travel. Comforts. I still had a good many payments left to make on it. . . . Leona asked me, for her sake, to put it up as security for a fifty-thousand-dollar loan from the bank. . . . How could I refuse? We gave him the money. He said he would send money every month, until the loan was repaid. He didn't. There was always a reason that he couldn't. And the payments on both loans were becoming impossible to meet.

"Leona knew what the Guarnerius meant to me. She decided to go on a European concert tour in order to pay off

Noel's loan. I argued, I pleaded, I said I would find the money somehow. But she knew there was no other way to get it, and she was immovable once she'd made a decision. She said she felt responsible, she said she couldn't bear it if I lost the Guarnerius.

"She was three months pregnant. We'd waited a long time for a child.

"In Israel . . ."

His heavy-lidded eyes looked out from their shadows, bleak and haunted.

"In Israel she was killed by a terrorist bomb."

I felt myself shivering uncontrollably. Mirisch looked away, into the garden. Greenfield looked down at the ground.

"I couldn't play after that. I just couldn't play any more. I couldn't even listen to music. . . . I stopped working. There was no money coming in. I finally had to put the Guarnerius up for sale.

". . . I hated him. Implacably. He was a spoiler. He was one of those . . . amoral . . . creatures who never consider other people's lives, who know nothing but the satisfaction of their own needs.

"He was on the coast when she died. In Palm Springs. He somehow couldn't get back to be with his parents. They both died before the year was out. Within six months of each other. He married shortly after that. I never met his wife. I don't think she ever knew about me, or about the Guarnerius.

"I didn't see him for sixteen years. For a long time I had nothing to do with music, went to no concerts. I accepted a job from a cousin who worked for a publishing firm. I lived alone. I didn't want to marry again. About ten years ago I got a check from him, for fifty thousand dollars. I sent it to the Israel Philharmonic. What else would I do with it now?

"Last fall I heard that he had joined the BSO. Six months later I read there was a del Gesù at Sotheby's in New York. I went to New York to see it. It was my violin. I knew it the way I know my own house, my own pillow. I was late. The

auction had already taken place. The man in charge told me
the name of the man who had acquired it . . .

". . . I thought I would kill him then.

"But I called him, instead. I said 'I believe you have my
Guarnerius. I would like to have it.' He laughed. He pretended not to know what I was saying. He was bland,
charming. He said I was welcome to come and play it any
time.

"Killing is anathema to me, but I knew I would kill him.
Not only for what he had done to me, but for what he was.
What he was part of. The society of the anti-human. People
who walk and talk and function as humans do, except that
they have no reverence for life, no interest in the true nature
of love, no horror of the brutal, the ugly, the sterile. They
have only that—*lethal* indifference to consequences, that—
murderous dismissal of the importance of anything that
doesn't serve their personal goals. The money addicts. The
power addicts . . . The terrorists . . ."

He swallowed. He shook his head.

"I took a life—with poison." He looked up. "Would you
care to estimate how many lives, every hour of every day,
are being taken—with poison—*sanctioned* poison—*ration-
alized* poison—better known as calculated risk, the eu-
phemism of the lobbyists and the government agencies who
look the other way?

"Ask the men who run the chemical plants, and the nu-
clear plants, the farmers who feed their livestock with car-
cinogens and the men who spray their crops with them—ask
them to judge a man accused of taking a life with poison,
and they'll be the first to convict him.

"But who convicts *them?* Who would convict Damaskin
for taking the lives of my wife and child with his poisonous
self-interest? *Subtle* murder, you see, goes unpunished.

"I can't kill them all. But at least I've struck back, *once*.
They'll have to listen to me—*once*."

He coughed, took a deep breath, and was silent.

Greenfield looked down at the lumpy handkerchief in his
hand. "If you were making a point," he said quietly, "then

why all the subterfuge? Why the broken deck, and the rest of the scare tactics? If you were making a point, why throw everyone off the scent?"

"I wanted time. I wanted to be free long enough to—to reclaim a fraction of those lost years."

I spoke before I knew I was going to, and my voice was husky, as though I'd just woken up. "I don't understand how you could destroy Mr. Holchek's garden."

The deep-set eyes looked up at me, puzzled. "Garden? I don't know anything about a garden. Why would I destroy a *garden?*"

Greenfield stood and pocketed the handkerchief. "There's no shortage of vandals," he said. "What did you do with the rest of the poison?"

Mirisch shook his head and smiled his sweet, sad smile.

"No," he said, standing, "there was no more. And if there had been, I wouldn't have kept it for myself. It would defeat the purpose."

Greenfield took a few harassed steps away and a few back. "Koussevitzky," he said, "is credited with having said that counterpoint is a Talmudic concept—the ability to argue two opposing points of view simultaneously. Killing is anathema, but destroying the killer is acceptable. The Talmud—and the courts—have something in common. Not much, but something. You—unfortunately—will be a victim of your own contrapuntal views. I applaud your humanity. I deplore its consequences. The rules are the rules. They're all we have, at the moment."

"Half an hour," Mirisch said.

Greenfield looked at him steadily. "I never let anything interfere with a concert," he said, "if I can help it."

Mirisch set off down the path at a good pace, and we watched him go.

"Damn it," I said, "I don't have any Kleenex."

"I'd offer you my handkerchief, but I'm afraid it's occupied—and possibly lethal."

We walked out of the formal garden and I ran in through the door marked "Women" at the back of the Main House, grabbed a fistful of toilet paper, and blew my nose, and then we made our way across the lawn filled with sitting and reclining concertgoers, toward the Music Shed. I thought I knew what was going to happen, but I wasn't certain.

We had no seats for that performance, only lawn tickets, so we stood at the back of the Shed, behind the audience.

The orchestra was already onstage. The audience was pleasantly anticipatory, removing raincoats, murmuring over the program, congratulating themselves on the fact that the sky had cleared in time for their evening's entertainment. The Ravel was the opening work; I'd forgotten it was being played that night. I wasn't certain I could bear to hear it.

The audience grew silent.

Seconds before Sorrel appeared, a man came through the stage right entrance carrying a violin, his dress conforming precisely to that of the other musicians, made his way to the empty seat next to Holchek, and sat down as though he had every right to be there.

It was Mirisch, with the Guarnerius.

Musicians glanced at one another, stirred in their seats. Shura half-rose from his chair, there was the beginning of a murmur in the audience, but there was no time for reaction to set in. Sorrel appeared, applause broke out, Sorrel bowed and turned to the orchestra.

There was a single, shocked moment as he caught sight of Mirisch. Confusion stopped his baton in mid-air, then he made a choice. The baton moved. The music began.

F-sharp, E, D, C-sharp, over and over and over, a soft, mesmeric spume of music.

The bow of the Guarnerius was perfectly synchronized with those of the other violins. Mirisch looked serene.

I wondered what had flashed through Sorrel's mind. That someone had sent in a substitute without consulting him? That he'd seen the man before, in some other context? And the other musicians? They no longer seemed apprehensive, they were given over to the music. Timing was everything. Mirisch had simply walked in through the locker rooms and onto the stage at precisely the moment of optimum advantage.

I looked around at the audience. It was as though some all-pervading benison had descended from the rafters and enveloped them. These were the same faces you could see on any street, in any shop, over any desk or counter, sharp with stress, furrowed with anxiety, contorted, as my friend would say, by the thousand shocks that flesh is heir to. But here, thanks to the ineffable beauty of the music, thanks to the hundred and seven artists on that stage, not a single face showed signs of daily battle. Here they were content. Here they were part of something excellent and imperishable.

This was part of what Mirisch wanted to preserve. What he took a life, and gave his life, to preserve.

The police were out there. The evidence was in Greenfield's pocket. And the criminal, while waiting for capture, was playing Ravel. The "Rapsodie" ended. Applause thundered from the audience. Sorrel bowed. And Mirisch rose and left the stage. No one stopped him.

I turned away, toward the lawn, and saw a duplication of Eleanor Springer. Jenny was sitting on the wet grass, motionless, with tears trickling down her face.

I said to Greenfield, "I have to go back. I'm tired. I want to pack my things. I'm leaving in the morning." .

He sighed, a man accustomed to bearing crosses.

"I have to stay. I want Shura to know he no longer has anything to worry about—and to tell the rest of the orchestra. I imagine," he added carefully, "I can get Shura to drive me back."

He knew damn well he could. I wasn't too worried about his transportation problems; there were always people going back and forth between Wheatleigh and Tanglewood. And taxis. Not to mention those two limbs we were given for the purpose of getting around.

When I left Wheatleigh the next morning, the sun was out and the day was already beginning to heat up. Jenny had talked her mother into going to Arrowhead with her to look at Melville's house. Sorrel and his wife were gone. The three old people were on the terrace arguing about whether or not Koussevitzky's grave overlooked Tanglewood. The tennis quartet was loading up two station wagons, preparing to depart, the Felkers were consulting a brochure about Shaker country, the new arrivals, soon to be the old arrivals, were off on a buying spree to Stockbridge. And a family with two prepubescent children was checking in.

Greenfield, standing under the ornate marquee of the porte cochere, holding the William Manchester book and looking as though he anticipated being restless in the near future, had decided to let me drop him off at Tanglewood on my way to Route 7. When the beard had stowed my bag inside the hatchback and said with genuine warmth that I must be sure to come back, Greenfield got in beside me, scrutinizing my cheerless countenance from under his unkempt eyebrows, and I drove out of the Countess's courtyard and down past the tennis court.

"You're upset," he said accusingly.

"Oh no," I protested glumly, "God's in his heaven and all's hunky-dory with the world."

He sighed. "I don't know when you're going to stop being surprised. What happened to Mirisch is not unique. People who see life systematically being robbed of everything that makes it bearable, frequently become dangerous."

"Why not? I've had a few homicidal urges myself after reading about the movers and shakers in the morning *Times*."

"The movers and shakers," Greenfield said, "come in all shapes and sizes, and they're immune to retaliation and blind to warning signs. None of them understands what Ulysses was saying." He paused, waiting for me to admit ignorance, then realized I wouldn't, and went on. "The Shakespearean coup de grâce to the whole business, Troilus and Cressida: *Take but degree away, untune that string, and, hark, what discord follows.*"

I pulled up at the Lion's Gate. *Untune that string.*

"Fortunately for last night's concert," he went on, "the

K47

Guarnerius was in tune. Unfortunately for Damaskin, Mirisch wasn't. Discord followed."

"An untuned string," I murmured. "My God, that man knew everything."

Greenfield got out of the car.

"He probably even knew," he said, "that the movers and shakers are tone deaf and couldn't care less about discord." And he went off through the gate onto the Tanglewood grounds.

14

I PARKED in front of the old white mansard-roofed house and went in. I could hear Calli and Helen in the downstairs office arguing about who had last seen a supply of paper clips. I stuck my head in and said hello.

Calli, berry-brown, whooped and said she couldn't wait to tell me about her vacation. Helen, red and peeling, looked sympathetic and said what a shame it was that I'd had to spend the two weeks doing the same old thing.

"Well," I said, "what with one thing and another, it wasn't all that dull."

I went upstairs to the Collier brothers' hangout.

Greenfield was standing at his desk removing items from a brown paper Rexall bag. He'd been driven home by his daughter Julie who had returned from New Mexico just in time to get off the plane and into her car and drive to Massachusetts.

Greenfield had called to tell me that justice being what it is, Mirisch would probably go to prison, but that he seemed strangely buoyant and said he was going to write a book.

I watched while he took the last of the items from the paper bag. There were twelve of them. All Cutter's.

"*Twelve?*" I said.

"I've decided to keep one permanently in my suitcase."

"And the other eleven?"

He sat down comfortably in the noisy swivel chair, took

off his glasses, and looked with melancholy satisfaction at a blue jay eating the crumbs on the windowsill.

"It's not inconceivable," he said, "that the idiots will stop manufacturing it."